AN ACCOMPLICE AGAINST TIME

Jennifer L. Kelly

This is a work of fiction. All of the characters, organizations, and events portrayed in this novel are either products of the author's imagination or are used fictitiously.

DEDICATION

To my sister from another mister, Nancy.

2101
PARIS, FRANCE

The snow swirled in an eddy at her feet as Maeve hurried down the sidewalk, her heeled boots making an audible noise like a gunshot with each firm step. Streetlamps splashed pools of light along her path at regular intervals. Above, the moon was full and the clouds were swollen with unfallen snow. They cast an ethereal glow across the night sky.

Under normal circumstances, she'd think it was a beautiful winter's night. But these were not normal circumstances. She pulled her brown fur coat tighter around her shoulders, shivering against the night air. As she walked the city shifted. The streetlamps became sparser. Some no longer burned, the oil having been neglected. Every one of her senses was on high alert. The sound of a train echoed in the distance. Old buildings made of stone and brick seemed to leer over her. She held her breath as she passed a bundle of cloth piled in an entryway. A dirty dish with a few coins in it indicated that the bundle was a person. She tucked her chin deeper into her coat. She was almost there. A cat screeched from a nearby alley way, and she couldn't help but wonder if it was an omen of what was to come.

A man was approaching on the sidewalk, his hat low over his eyes and hands shoved into his pockets. Her eyes swiftly scanned him, taking in his tailored wool coat and the cashmere scarf wound round his neck. The shining black boots that crunched over the snow. There was a single red rose in the lapel of his coat. It stood out in stark contrast to their surroundings—something beautiful and alive where so little beauty remained.

He lifted his chin slightly and she saw that he had piercing sapphire blue eyes. Just as he seemed about to say something to her, the words died on his lips as slender fingers reached out and grabbed her arm, jerking her to the right and pulling her into the safety of a nearby doorway.

"There you are!" hissed the voice. It was female and it was annoyed. Elaina was always annoyed. "What in Heaven's name took you so long?"

Maeve took a moment to peer back around the doorway. The man was gone.

"Nothing took me so long. I'm here, aren't I?"

Elaina looked at what appeared to be a watch, but Maeve knew it was not. Sure, it kept time. But also kept multiple locations, dates, and time zones. To an untrained eye though, it simply looked like a very elegant time piece.

"He's about to speak in ten minutes. Come on." Elaina grabbed Maeve and pulled her out of the doorway and along the sidewalk, making a left into an alley way lined with trash bins and debris. A rat scuttled out of the way. They walked until they reached an arched entry in between two of the buildings. If one was just walking down the alley, it likely would be overlooked. It was very narrow; a larger man would have to turn sideways to walk down it. As it was, the two women moved quickly through the arch and down the alley. A small lantern beckoned in the distance.

Here, the buildings blocked the snow, but the shadowed chill was even worse. Maeve could hear the deep tenors of an argument emanating from the buildings above them. She heard a car horn honk half-heartedly.

Elaina finally came to a stop at a door painted black—almost invisible unless you knew where to look. She tried the handle. It was locked. Giving Maeve a knowing smile, she removed one of her leather gloves and reached into her curled coiffure. She pulled out a long hair pin and proceeded to jam it into the key slot of the handle's lock. When she tried the handle this time the door swung silently open. Elaina dropped the hairpin into the pocket of her wool coat and pulled her glove back on. She looked over her shoulder at Maeve and put a finger to her lips.

When she turned back around Maeve rolled her eyes. That was the annoying thing about Elaina. She always acted like she was the one in charge and that she knew more than everyone else. Which in this case, was actually not the case. Elaina was simply the point of entry. She wouldn't be admitted into the room where the speech was to occur. Her role was to hang out at the bar and eavesdrop, gossip, and flirt with the staff and other attendees hoping someone who had overly imbibed or who couldn't resist a pretty face would reveal some tantalizing bit of much needed information.

They moved down a narrow unlit corridor. The air was cool, and they were moving downward as if heading toward the basement of the building they'd entered. When Elaina came to a sudden stop, Maeve stopped too but not before her chin jutted painfully into Elaina's shoulder. Even though it was pitch black, she was pretty sure Elaina glared at her.

Elaina started forward again as she pushed open a wooden door. It let out a creak of protest and Maeve held her breath, but soon realized as they stepped over the threshold that the sound was lost in the bustle of a kitchen.

Busboys carrying large, round trays maneuvered around cooks yelling instructions and women washing dishes in a large concrete sink, their faces pink and perspiring. A young boy was polishing silverware near where they had entered, and he gave them an unsurprised look. He pointed to a curtain behind him. Elaina gave him a nod and dropped a handful of coins into his open palm. No one even seemed to notice them as they slipped past the curtain and up the wooden stairs.

The din of people dining and conversing drifted down to them and the oddly appropriate notes of *Claire du Lune* swallowed them as they reached the top of the stairs. There was a small room directly in front of them; it had a counter and a little silver bell with a long handle. No one appeared amongst the racks of furs, tweeds, and wool. To the right was a hallway where the piano melody drifted down the hallway. To the left was another hallway marked by a large crystal chandelier and lined with magnificent gaslit sconces. Maeve was glad that this time she had not overdressed for the occasion.

They deposited their coats and gloves not at the coat check, but in a nearby broom closet for easier retrieval.

In the dim light Elaina's blonde hair sparkled with jeweled pins that complemented her sparkling champagne evening gown. The gown was beautiful. It had delicate beaded straps and the dress fell in a cascade of shimmering crystal-encrusted tulle over Elaina's curvy figure. She looked down at her time piece, a slim gold bracelet that accentuated the delicate bones of her wrist and pursed her red lips.

"You only have a couple of minutes. Go!" She gave Maeve a gentle shove in the direction of the chandelier and when Maeve glanced back, the other girl was already gone, the click of her high heels fading in the distance.

Maeve took a deep breath. Where Elaina was light, Maeve was dark. Her dark hair was rolled in voluminous curls past her shoulders. Her light hazel eyes were framed with dark lashes and her porcelain skin was complimented by the green velvet gown she had chosen for this mission. She smoothed her full skirts nervously, and her own time piece slid down her wrist—a silver bangle encrusted with small emeralds—one minute.

She hurried down the hallway, her heeled boots were hidden beneath her dress. Practical shoes were one thing on which she was unwilling to compromise. Satin slippers could be the difference between life and death.

At the end of the hallway was a set of carved ivory double doors. The scrolls and flowers were exquisite, but the excessiveness of the source made Maeve's stomach clench. How many elephants gave their lives for this door? There was opulence, then there was opulence beyond reason. This was the latter.

A butler stood near the doorway. He didn't make eye contact but offered her a flute of champagne from his tray. She accepted, tilted her head in thanks, and sipped her champagne as another butler with tousled brown hair appeared from seemingly out of nowhere and hurried to open the giant doors. As she glided past him, she caught his eye, and he gave her the slightest of winks before closing the door behind her.

The room was dimly lit and before her were tables and chairs full of people. Men and women dressed in their finest. The cacophony of voices and clink of glasses immediately relaxed her. Noise equaled invisibility. At the front of the room was a stage flanked on either side by heavy, dark curtains. A spotlight shone down onto the center of the stage from above, creating a perfect pool of golden light. She made her way along the edge of the room's back wall, her back slightly turned so that if anyone came up from behind her, she'd still be able to see them.

As she moved around the room, she glanced into each of the alcoves that were spaced around the perimeter. The spaces were ideal for private conversations, business deals and other things she thought darkly. Some were unoccupied, others had the curtains pulled. Still others held people who didn't mind being seen together but wanted to step away from the din of the other partygoers. At one end of the room was a triple set of French doors, presumably leading out to manicured gardens for a snowy moonlit stroll or breath of fresh air. The middle set of doors were open, allowing the wintry breeze to circulate around the room. Maeve did appreciate that. These gowns could be quite heavy, add into that stays or a corset and it became downright claustrophobic, so the cool breeze felt refreshing.

She selected the second alcove from the garden doors and took a step back into the darkness just as a man walked onto the stage and into the spotlight. Immediately the audience grew quiet, and Maeve could feel the anticipation in the air.

The man was shorter than average, and his waistcoat was snug around his rotund waist. He wore wire frame glasses, and his sparse hair was unattractively combed over his balding head. In contrast, his mustache was quite bushy and hung over his mouth like a bloated gray rat resting on his upper lip. It was hard to believe this man could command such silence that one could hear a pin drop, but as it was, Maeve knew him to be one of the most dangerous men in history which made her stomach turn once more. She set her champagne flute down on the alcove's table. *Get the message and then get the hell out*, she reminded herself.

"Ladies and gentlemen, thank you for your attendance this evening. I will not beat around the bush as they say. Indeed, we are all here for the same reason. Without further ado, I introduce to you our visionary leader who in actuality truly needs no introduction."

At that people immediately began to clap and some even got to their feet. A tall, slender man entered from stage left. As the spotlight found him, Maeve could see that he had sable hair with just the slightest hint of white at his temples and an angular face with an aquiline nose. He moved with the grace of a dancer as he made his way across the stage. His suit was a crisp navy and immaculately cut to fit every curve of muscle in his lean body. He clasped hands with the short man who puffed out his chest proudly. Maeve felt her lip involuntarily curl in response.

As the shorter man disappeared into the blackness surrounding the stage, the tall man gave a closed-lipped smile and made a motion for the audience to resume their seats, which they all immediately did. His tie was the same emerald as her dress and Maeve felt her skin prickle as she studied him. The audience waited with bated breath for him to speak. He looked out over the crowd taking them in as though he was breathing in their anticipation and savoring it. His eyes landed on her and she realized with a start that they were a piercing sapphire blue—just like the man she had passed on the street. His lips curled in a soft smile of recognition. But that's impossible, Maeve thought. *He cannot recognize me in the dark. Surely, he's blinded by the stage lighting.* As quickly as he'd seemed to notice her, his eyes continued to rove over the room in self-satisfaction. Once his eyes were off her, Maeve realized that she was trembling. If the other man was one of the most dangerous in history, then this man was *the* most dangerous in all of time—in any direction.

***

Sebastian Bates was a charismatic career politician. Women loved him with his debonair looks and deceptive boyish grin. Men wanted to be him because he oozed wealth and power from every pore of his being. His aspirations were not just big; they were totalitarian. He was not satisfied to be leader of a single country, nor even of an entire continent. Sebastian would not stop until he was leader of the entire civilized world. In this opulent ballroom, his worst crimes had yet to be committed.

Maeve picked up her champagne and downed it in a single gulp. The young butler who had opened the door for her earlier, sidled over to her. He had been standing, invisibly against the damask-covered wall, holding a tray of champagne flutes. She gratefully accepted one, feeling her trembling subside as the fizziness filled her head. Her rule was never more than two drinks. In her line of work keeping your wits about you was another difference between life and death.

"Makes your skin crawl, doesn't he?"

"You make my skin crawl, Marco," she replied taking a long sip of her champagne.

The butler grinned at her his brown eyes warm with admiration. "Keep whispering sweet nothings to me, darling." Before they could attract any unwanted attention, he strolled away.

Maeve realized that she was no longer trembling, and she felt like she had regained some control over her initial fear of Sebastian recognizing her. Truly, it was near impossible…No, it was *completely* impossible.

The crowd had settled down after their raucous ovation. They now sat rapt with attention staring up at Sebastian who was about to deliver his victory speech at the ball that was being held in his honor; thrown by his own humble self.

She sipped her champagne and stared out into the dimly lit dining area. Men in dapper suits with waistcoats and ties; women draped in diamonds, gems and even circlets or tiaras. Maeve knew that even though Sebastian had plenty of his own wealth—as evidenced by the building in which she now stood—it didn't prevent the world's most wealthy families and individuals from donating even more to Sebastian's political career. His aspirations were their aspirations.

Finally, he spoke.

"Tonight is not just a victory for me. It's a victory for all of us." The audience clapped appreciatively. Their money had been well spent. The propaganda machine had been in overdrive this election; continually bombarding people with false and misleading headlines across all of the newspapers.

Step one, censor the dissidents. Step two, hold the population captive through fear mongering. Step three, propagandize the now vulnerable population into the desired action. When one can't question the truth, it makes it very easy to be manipulated. Did these donors and supporters even know that their money went straight into Project Echo?

"The people have spoken. They are ready for a new frontier. A frontier that promises a future of innovation and prosperity." *Yeah, not for regular people,* snorted Maeve to herself. She took another sip of her champagne. "They are ready to move forward and embrace change—change that only we can offer them. A life where everyone knows their role..."

"And everyone knows their place!" chorused the audience finishing the line for him. Maeve's skin broke out into goosebumps. People like Maeve had certainly been shown their place.

Sebastian's smile widened. His face was clean shaven and unlined despite his salt and pepper hair. His shoulders were wide and even though his frame was slim and muscular, Maeve knew that his physical strength was even more prolific than his mental aptitude. An indefatigable soldier. A perfect leader.

He gestured as if to encompass the crowd. "And your place as my generous donors! Your role as the future leaders of our reimagined society!"

"More like oligarchy," a voice whispered. Marco had come back and was standing to her right. She glared at him, and he disappeared with his empty tray, probably through a hidden door that led back to the bar area for him to replenish his tray. Maeve didn't doubt that copious amounts of champagne would be drunk that night.

Sebastian continued. "We still have much work to do. But I do not doubt that together, we can conquer our opposition and move forward into the bright future that awaits us all." The audience applauded heartily, and he tilted in a slight bow of acknowledgement.

That was oddly short, Maeve thought to herself. Then again it was only a victory party. But there was clearly no message hidden within the brief speech. Maybe Elaina had had better luck.

As Sebastian straightened, confetti of black, silver, and gold fell from the ceiling showering the stage. A young girl of maybe twelve wearing a white dress of sparkles, tulle and satin was nudged toward the stage. She was holding a bunch of red roses and held them up to Sebastian. He leaned over patting the girl on her head of tawny ringlets. The confetti had stopped falling but coated his hair and his shoulders. From the girl's bouquet, he extracted a single rose. Confused, the girl held the remaining flowers to her chest and turned back toward the crowd.

Theatrically, Sebastian inhaled the scent of the rose. Eyes closed, lips upturned in the hint of a smile. When he opened his eyes, he said simply, "To victory." As the crowd echoed his sentiment, his sapphirine eyes locked on Maeve's once again and he held the rose up and out in her direction, as if he were toasting her. There was no mistaking it this time. The message was in fact for her.

***

Maeve pulled her fur coat tightly around her as she took deep breaths. A broom was jabbing into her rib cage, and she was sitting atop a haphazard jumble of empty crates. Near the door, an unlit lantern hung on the wall casting her in darkness. This was the janitorial closet where she and Elaina had hidden their coats earlier that evening because she could no longer stand to be in that ball room a moment longer. Not with those sapphire eyes.

There was a gentle knock on the door and her heart froze in her chest before a voice softly said her name. She reached out—as that's all the space there was—and pushed open the door. Marco stepped inside and shut the door silently behind him. He was still wearing his butler uniform—shirtsleeves, silver brocade waistcoat, navy tie and matching black pants and jacket—but he had abandoned his tray of champagne flutes. But apparently not the champagne, he held a bottle in his hand and extended it to her.

She immediately took it and drank a healthy swig eyeing him warily over the bottle.

Marco could be annoying because he constantly flirted with all the female agents, but he was also incredibly sweet when it came down to it. He was kind and he was also fairly harmless, and more often than she cared to count did he not only get them into a jam, but also was the one to get them out of it. He was much more resourceful as a partner than Elaina ever was.

"How did you know?" she asked as she handed the bottle back to him.

"I was working the coat check before the evening began and then switched to the butler role once dinner began. Poor chap who had the champagne tray during cocktails suddenly came down with a bump on the head and a bit of a fainting spell. Sent him home for the night." Marco took the bottle and held it to his own mouth, his warm brown eyes considering her.

She knew he had done that for her. He wasn't supposed to be in that room with her. She was supposed to be in there alone.

"He's a creep, you know. The way he looks at you…"

She did know. In one timeline she had thought she could love a young Sebastian Bates, but that felt like many timelines ago.

"He's egotistical," she replied simply. *But he wasn't always that way,* she continued the thought to herself.

"Oh, believe me, I know. But Porter is much worse. And more cruel. I have the scars to prove it." Marco's expression darkened and Maeve shuddered again.

"Hey," he said setting the bottle of champagne onto a dusty shelf. "Let's get out of here. Elaina should be done about now." Maeve nodded. Elaina would stop to pick up her coat and notice Maeve's own coat was no longer there and understand that she and Marco had already left to meet at their rendezvous point.

Marco pulled the lantern from the wall, lit it, and handed it to Maeve who blocked its golden light with the palm of her hand. He cracked open the door and peered out into the lobby.

"All clear. I'll see you there." He slipped out and when Maeve peered out, he was already gone. She set the lantern back into its iron holder on the wall and peered into the lobby again. A butler hurried past her carrying a full tray of champagne flutes. So intent on his mission—and performance—that he didn't notice the young woman peeking curiously out of the doorway.

She slipped out and silently made her way down the marble steps and out the grand doorway that led onto the city street. Once outside, she immediately breathed in the cold night air. The champagne had warmed her, and her mind was fuzzy around the edges. Her body felt like it was crackling with energy.

The snow had really picked up and already coated the sidewalk and street in a blanket of white. The entrance to La Plaza rested on the main thoroughfare and across the way was Le Jardin. Once she crossed the street, she just had to cross through the gardens to the other side. There was a pub there named Le Temps and the attic of Le Temps was the rendezvous point for this particular mission.

She stepped off the sidewalk and felt firm fingers grab her wrist. She wasn't wearing any gloves and the fingers were warm. She knew before she turned around who it was that gripped her.

He whirled her around to face him.

The snow was coming down quickly and coated the shoulders of his expensive navy suit, but he didn't seem to either mind nor care. His sapphire eyes were ablaze, not with anger, but amusement.

"I never thought I'd see you again."

His voice was deep and tinged with some emotion she couldn't quite identify. It was not the charismatic voice of an alter ego that had spoken from that small stage only moments ago.

She didn't know what to say. This man standing before her had yet to commit the sins she knew he was going to commit. He also was no longer the young man she had loved all those years ago. Years for him anyways. For her the wound was still fresh enough to reopen easily.

He considered her. "You haven't changed, not one bit." His other arm had slipped around her waist so easily she hadn't even noticed. They were chin to chin as he gazed down at her. To anyone passing by they would simply look like a couple on the sidewalk enjoying a romantic embrace in the snow.

She finally found her voice. "I cannot say the same for you, Sebastian. You've changed quite a lot since the last time I saw you." It was a petty thing to say, but she couldn't help herself. Her heart ached at the sight of him.

"Blunt as ever," he murmured, but he was smiling. That dazzling perfect smile that belied what he was truly thinking or feeling. The smile that distracted people from the truth.

"You don't look a day over twenty-four," he said running a finger gently along her cheek. Instead of shivering she felt a heat spread across her chest and rise up her neck. He was only twenty-eight the last time she had seen him. It had been over a decade for him; but only months for her.

"I have to go," she said resisting the urge to lean into his touch and instead pulling slightly back.

"Ah. A rendezvous, eh? Well, now I know you are still interested. And that I will see you again." He lowered his face to hers and kissed her deeply. She responded instinctively. The mental barrier broke and the sensations and memories from the past came rushing back into her. He was the one to break the kiss, pulling away slowly. Reluctantly. "After all these years, I can wait a little longer. À bientôt, my darling Maeve."

He released her and stepped swiftly back into the doorway of La Place—his building in his city. It was representative of everything he was working to build. It took a second for her to regain her equilibrium. Her head and her heart were both spinning. His sudden release of her had taken with it the rush of warmth and she now shivered despite her fur coat. Her instinct was to run and put as much distance between her and Sebastian as possible. Between herself and those memories. Could she outrun the past? Instead, she held her head high and stepped off the curb and onto the snow-covered street carefully making her way across to Le Jardin. Also, *his* garden. He owned many of the rebuilt cities. At the scrolled iron archway marking the entrance to the gardens, she finally got the nerve to turn around and look back. He was still standing there in the shadows of the entrance to La Place, watching her. His eyes were unreadable at this distance, but she could see an unmistakable small smile on his perfectly curved lips. She turned into the park and began to run.

***

"What took you so long? I thought you were right behind me."

Marco already had the fireplace lit when she arrived. He was huddled around it; he'd changed out of his butler uniform and now wore a ragged jacket, dirty hole-ridden wool scarf, pants with smudges of soot and a worn knit cap. If they dressed like beggars, it was easier to remain invisible in the streets of a city like Paris. *You could never be invisible to me.* Sebastian's deep voice reverberated through her mind. She shook her head to clear it.

She slipped out of her fur coat, tossing it onto a dust-sheet-covered sofa and turned her back to Marco. He immediately stepped away from the fire and began quickly unbuttoning the back of her dress. Once, she'd found this action to be unbearably intimate—memories of other fingers smoothly doing and undoing the buttons—but she quickly learned having assistance was the only way to quickly change in and out of disguises, especially when the disguise involved era appropriate gowns and sometimes even the dreaded corsets.

Marco's fingers deftly undid the back of her dress down to her tailbone and then went to work on the ribbons of the corset. She quickly removed a few pins from her hair and shook out the long jet-black waves.

Once her corset was undone, she took in a deep breath of air. It hadn't been particularly tight, but it always felt good to be able to fully expand one's ribcage. Marco handed her a bundle of cloth and turned his back respectfully as she stepped out of the gown and into the trousers. Her booted feet fit through the wide leg openings because the pants were made for a boy. Women did not typically wear pants or even divided skirts in this era. Unless, of course, they wanted to stand out or were riding a bike. Neither of which Maeve desired to do. She slipped her arms through the shirtsleeves and began buttoning the front of the shirt. When she turned around Marco was shoving the beautiful green velvet dress into a large laundry sack. The fur coat was already gone and in its place was a ragged wool peacoat. It was peculiar to Maeve that fashions from centuries ago had once again gained in popularity particularly among the elite. Human fascinations would never cease to amaze or perplex her.

Marco looked up at her from his kneeling position, his eyebrow raised in question. She still hadn't answered him.

The door opening spared her the need to respond.

Elaina slipped into the room, the snow still fresh in her blonde hair. Immediately, she handed her coat to Marco like he was her personal valet. Maeve stepped forward and expertly began undoing the column of buttons down her back as she removed the jeweled pins from her hair.

"That was invigorating!" Elaina breathed as she stepped out of her dress and slipped into a pair of trousers. Her blue eyes sparkled, and she smelled of whiskey and cigar smoke.

"You always love a good party," Maeve replied handing her a button-down shirt. Elaina turned and Maeve undid her stays. Marco had slipped out of the room and now he returned with a bowl of water and some rags. He set them on an old sideboard that wobbled on the wood plank floor because one of its legs was shorter than the rest.

Marco produced a bar of soap and Maeve went to the bowl and began to wash the makeup from her face. When she was done, Marco went over to the small fireplace and ran his fingers along some of the stones before coming to her and smudging the soot on her face. Then he did the same for Elaina, but even the soot could not hide the excitement in her eyes. What had she found out?

Maeve pressed a button on her watch, and it shifted from gold to a dirty black band of cloth. She didn't want to tell her team that Sebastian had not only seen her, but that he had recognized her and followed her. The agency knew she had once been in love with Sebastian—it's why she had been recruited in the first place. And once she had been told who he would become, it was the reason she had said yes to joining them.

Surely, though, if she told her teammates, Marco and Elaina would report the incident to their superior, and she'd be removed from the mission. Then again, maybe she wouldn't be removed from the mission. An agent who knew Sebastian as well as she did and who could get intimately close to him without suspicion…Although Sebastian would naturally be suspicious. A man like him was always suspicious of everyone, no matter how intimately involved.

She hadn't realized she was still standing in the middle of the room lost in thought as Marco and Elaina had settled down on the dirty floor, opening tins of beans and meat and packages of crackers.

"Care to join us?" Elaina asked.

Marco gave her a curious look as she knelt down next to him and peeled back the lid on a tin of beans. From the kitchen Marco had snuck out three bottles of beer which they gratefully drank while they ate with their fingers.

"What I wouldn't give for a bite of that filet mignon they served tonight. And a hot buttered roll. It smelled divine in there!" Even with soot on her face, dressed like a street urchin and speaking with her mouthful, Elaina was beautiful. And yet still annoying.

Marco scowled at her. "Doth speak too much."

Her smile vanished and she scowled at him. "Well, you two don't speak at all! It's like working with two stone monoliths!"

"Some people are better at observing, Elaina. Others are better at talking. You fall into the latter. That's why you're so good at your assignments."

Maeve was used to Elaina's teasing, but she often found her colleague behaved in childish ways. She was a flirt and quite beautiful which was why her assignments often involved social situations where she could potentially overhear, or in some cases be outright told by a flirtatious soldier or politician who had had too much to drink, critical information. Many men could not resist a pretty face, especially if that pretty face was also willing to kiss them. Which Elaina was.

Elaina didn't notice the hidden criticism in Maeve's remarks.

"Let's debrief then before we go back to headquarters," Marco took a swig of his beer. Maeve was well aware that *he* was well aware that she had never answered his question.

"Mostly, I heard the usual. There were a few government officials in the lounge. Naturally, I was invited to sit on the arm of one of the provincial prime minister's chairs as a beautiful ornamentation." Humility was not one of Elaina's character traits. This sometimes got her into trouble. Like the time on her second mission, she thought she had won over an opposition soldier who took her home with him, thinking he'd spill secrets over an intimate evening, but instead he locked her in the closet and disappeared. Because she hadn't followed protocol and informed them in any way that she was deviating from the mission, they hadn't been able to locate her for hours. Until finally one of the barmaids admitted to seeing them leave and knew where the soldier was staying.

"They were extra celebratory because of this most recent victory. No one had expected Sebastian winning all of France would be so easy. Apparently, they didn't even have to cheat like they did in the provincial elections."

"Anything else?" Marco asked.

"Not particularly. One commissioner mentioned his general was moving soldiers to Belgium."

"That's not surprising, because we already know his next move is all of Europe."

"He'll have to overthrow each Prime Minister or President and install his own. That is going to take time," Elaina pointed out.

"Time that we don't have if we are going to alter the timeline," Marco said.

The Opus Mission was altering the past so that Sebastian would never be able to take global power. This involved smaller missions that created various pivot points in his timeline to power. The current mission was simply reconnaissance. Partly to gauge the mood after Sebastian's victory in France and partly to see if they could learn how quickly he planned to move into other countries in Europe. It wasn't as simple as knowing a date in the future—which they did—but being able to create subtle, unsuspecting changes along the way with the ultimate goal of derailing his pinnacle goal of global power.

"What about you, Marco?"

He took another swig of beer before answering. "It was the usual. All the donors were feeling particularly smug and I'm sure they threw millions more into the campaign. It's shocking how little he needs to say or do and they simply fawn all over him."

"What about in the kitchens?" asked Elaina.

"That's what was strange. Most of the servants seemed excited and even hopeful."

Maeve took a drink of her beer and nodded. "That seems right though. Right now, Sebastian is running on hope. France has been in a bad way since the Third World War and his policies offer them a glimpse into potential prosperity."

Elaina shook her head wistfully. "If they only knew his real intentions."

Maeve shrugged. "Hope for change can make people do strange things—if they're desperate enough."

"I don't understand how they can't see right through him," Marco said. His brow was lowered in a scowl.

"It's because he's so handsome and charming," Elaina said with a small smile. Maeve felt her stomach give a little tug as she recalled Sebastian's lips pressed to hers.

"No, it's not only that."

Marco looked up at her, his brow softening.

She continued, "Yes, he's handsome and charming. But also, he means it. When he says he wants what is best for France, or Europe or the world, he actually means it. It's hard for people to see through what is essentially the truth. Sebastian is certainly many things, but a liar isn't one of them."

2091
NEW YORK CITY, UNITED STATES

Maeve stood on the curb staring up at the tall stone building. It was one of a handful of structures that had been rebuilt after the war. The city had been all but annihilated during the world war. It had been eighteen years—she was born just after the war had ended. As part of the Repopulation Initiative. Before the war had reached its catastrophic climax, a donor bank of millions of embryos had been flash-frozen and placed inside a freezer vault hidden in a concrete and steel bunker nearly half a mile underground. A decade after the war ended and the radiation had subsided, the surviving world leaders and scientists had decided it was time to begin repopulation. Surrogate volunteers for the initiative had been hand selected for their intellect, talents, skills and accomplishments before the war, which had to be quite remarkable because when they were chosen, many of the volunteers were young teenagers— young women who would still be fertile a decade later to have an embryo implanted in their womb and gestate a baby until its birth. The young girls were taken into government protection only days before the first nuclear bomb was dropped on the United States.

Maeve had been one of those Repopulation Initiative babies. She didn't remember her birthing mother's name. Some children remained with their birthing mothers and were even raised by them, but others that showed certain aptitudes were removed from their maternal connections and labeled government assets. They were moved to a facility in the remote corn fields of Ohio not unlike a boarding school—except it was full of boys and girls of various ages with unique talents and gifts. At least that's what she had been told once she was older. Maeve had been transferred to the facility when she was only five years old. The only recollection of her birthing mother was warm brown eyes and dark skin and a beautiful smile that sang the most beautiful lullabies and told the most beautiful stories to her surrogate daughter. Maeve often wondered if her love of reading came from her biological parents or her birthing mother.

Now back in the present, the entrance to the Bates Library of International Studies loomed over her. Flanking the doorway were two stone-faced guards dressed in fatigues and holding guns. Strange, she wondered, that a library should need military protection. She shrugged her shoulders and pulled the iron handle of one of the giant wooden doors.

As she crossed the threshold, she was greeted with a rush of warmth and golden light. Copper gas lanterns flanked either side of the spacious room and a massive stone fireplace stood before her with a roaring fire inside.

She'd been told that before the war, buildings had been built primarily out of steel, glass and concrete. But these materials were susceptible to destruction—namely, melting from the intense heat of the nuclear blasts and the subsequent collapse of the structures. Nuclear fallout wasn't the only concern after the war, for years chemicals from the old building materials and construction process had lingered in the air. She had also learned that electricity had been available all around the world before the war. Naturally, the electrical grid of every country that had such a luxury had been destroyed during the war. In fact, it was one of the first systems compromised.

In the center of the building, it was open all the way up, revealing at least ten floors of spacious mahogany balconies showcasing rows and rows of bookcases. Many books, like the stored embryos and crop seed vaults, had been meticulously stored and saved. While in the bunkers waiting for the radiation to subside and the world above to become safe for re-inhabitation once again, scribes had painstakingly copied thousands of pieces of literature. The Bates Library of International Studies was the first library of the rebuilt world on any continent. It held treasures in Latin, Greek, Spanish, Italian, English, Egyptian, French, Chinese and many languages Maeve had never even knew existed.

Along the wall to her left was a long mahogany desk with an inset of emerald green marble outfitted in brass accents. The library was dark and moody with deep navy walls and mahogany woods. It was the most beautiful building she had ever been in—and she'd only taken a few steps.

Gripping her worn leather satchel, she made her way over to the long desk. She had spotted a young man standing behind it. When she approached, she saw that he was sorting, stamping and cataloging a stack of books. A small placard behind him read Circulation Desk. He did not look up from his work.

Maeve politely cleared her throat, and the man looked up with a startled expression. He must have been so lost in his work that he hadn't heard her approach.

The man had brown hair which curled behind his ears and stuck out every which way. His tie was crooked, and his shirtsleeves were rolled up to his elbows, revealing sinewy forearms. His face and hands were smudged with what Maeve assumed to be ink. He was clean shaven and appeared to be around her age; eighteen or so. But she did find it difficult to guess because depending on the difficulties one experienced in life it did have a way of accelerating the aging process.

"May I help you?" he asked. His eyes were a warm, chocolate brown and his lips curved up in the faintest of smiles.

"Yes, I saw an advertisement in the paper for an open position here."

The man's smile widened. "Ah, yes. I believe that was for the cataloging position?" Maeve nodded. The man made his way around the desk through a small, wooden swinging door.

"As you can see," he gestured around them. "There are thousands if not hundreds of thousands of books needing catalogued. Not only do we need records of all of them, but since we are the only functioning library of this magnitude in the recreated world, we often loan books out by the hundreds. Meticulous record-keeping is of the utmost importance."

While he talked, they had begun walking. He led her across the main room and to a spiral staircase in the back corner. They ascended and Maeve noticed the intricacy of the carved scroll design of the staircase's railing. The magnitude of the library became even more apparent as they reached the upper most level, as she looked out over the center below, her breath caught in her throat.

The man noticed and his smile widened as he noted a fellow book lover. "It's quite spectacular, isn't it?"

Maeve turned to him and saw the same sense of wonder reflected in his eyes. "It's the most magnificent thing that I've ever seen."

She followed him down one of the balconies back toward the front of the building. There was a short hallway to the right with a single door at the end. Light poured in from windows on the left, creating small panes of light on the limestone floor. The wooden door at the end was slightly ajar.

The man knocked and called. "Sir, there's a young woman here interested in the cataloging position."

After a moment, a deep voice responded. "Splendid. Send her in, Marco."

Marco smiled at her. "Good luck. Although, I suspect you shan't be needing it." He tilted his head in farewell and headed back down the hallway, disappearing around a corner.

Maeve took a deep breath and pushed open the door to the room.

Behind the door was a large office, lined with windows on two sides. A fire blazed in the fireplace on one wall and a gaslit chandelier hung in the center of the room above an enormous mahogany desk that sat atop a luxurious Turkish rug. Exotic animal mounts and artwork she recognized as Impressionist dotted the walls. A marble bust of Alexander the Great sat on a pedestal to her left and a sleek black marble obelisk gold-capped and engraved with Egyptian hieroglyphs on its sides towered just over her head and to her right. It was an eclectic, yet beautiful arrangement of objects.

Her eyes found the man who had spoken standing behind his desk. He looked young (again she was terrible at guessing) and incredibly handsome with wavy sable hair and piercing sapphire blue eyes. She could tell his suit was expensive because it was cut to fit his body perfectly. His silver tie and cobalt blue waistcoat set off his eyes beautifully.

He smiled and gestured at one of the leather wingback chairs in front of his desk. "Welcome to the Bates Library of International Studies. Marco said you're interested in our cataloging position?"

Still standing, she pulled the newspaper, which had been folded to the precise Help Wanted ad, out of her leather satchel. She pointed, "Yes, it says here that a love of reading is one of the requirements, and I think I fit that requirement quite nicely."

She sat in the chair, and once she had, the man sat as well.

On the corner of his desk, there was a silver tray with a coffee pot. He looked at her and she nodded. He poured her a cup and handed it to her, then nudged the sugar and creamer in her direction. She poured in copious amounts of cream, so the black liquid turned a caramel color, and omitted sugar entirely. The man did not add either sugar nor cream to his coffee.

He leaned back in his chair. "Tell me more about your love for reading."

"Well, I know that books can be somewhat hard to come by. But in my schooling, I developed a love for fiction as a young girl and since then my interests have expanded into poetry, historical texts, religion, philosophy and much more."

"Where is it that you received your schooling?"

"Hartford School for Young Ladies, Sir." She had attended the School for Young Ladies after her formative years at the co-ed school in Ohio on a recommendation from her literature teacher.

"Ah, the nuns there are quite notorious for their rigorous academic syllabus. While at the Hartford School for Young Ladies, what were your favorite subjects? Aside from reading?"

"Aside from literature, history and philosophy."

"And your interest in this particular position? Aside from your passion for books? What else makes you qualified for such a role?"

Maeve wondered if he'd had any other applicants. The advertisement had been in the previous morning's paper and Maeve had pondered it throughout the day. It had seemed rather serendipitous to find such an opportunity so soon after relocating to the city

She set the newspaper into her lap and took a demure sip of her coffee. "My passion for reading will enable me to excel in the position, but the real reason that I am interested is because I would like to contribute to the reacquisition of knowledge. From what I understand, so much has been lost. The censorship and burnings of various books and libraries all over the world during the war, not to mention those books that were unable to be saved."

The man's bright eyes considered her from over the rim of his cup. "A man's worth is no greater than his ambitions."

He was quoting Marcus Aurelius to her. Perhaps it was a test of sorts because she had mentioned she was a lover of philosophy. Indeed, her ambitions were high for this position. The options given to women were not great in the rebuilding era. She could become a birthing mother, a maidservant or governess, a nun, a nurse, a teacher, or a number of any other low-paid positions. In her schooling she had learned that at one point in the not-so-distant past, women had gained near work equality with their male counterparts, alas, the war had set things back in time not only with technology but other areas of society as well. To get this position would mean a level of independence unknown to many of her modern counterparts.

She was quite familiar with the Roman philosopher Marcus Aurelius and his works, so she replied without hesitation: "To understand the true quality of people, you must look into their minds and examine their pursuits and aversions."

The man's eyes brightened, and he laughed, setting down his coffee cup atop some papers haphazardly scattered across his desk. "Quite right. Naturally then I must also ask you, what are your aversions?"

She looked around the room, taking in its opulence. He hadn't properly introduced himself, but she suspected that she knew the identity of her interviewer, and if she was correct, his wealth superseded that of the majority of the known world. In fact, he *was* the richest man in the world. And even after the war great wealth meant great power. Perhaps more than it ever had before.

"I can think of one aversion."

"Only one?" he smiled indulgently.

She ignored this and answered him truthfully. "Dependence. Frankly, I need this position. A woman of my birth, well, let's just say that while I am thankful, it is not a birth revered for its nobility. I have been fortunate to be encouraged throughout my life because of my intellect and curiosity, which is why I am here today. Having no family, my biggest aversion is to a life of dependency on other people for my well-being. This position will hopefully prevent me from that situation."

His smile faded and his eyes took on a sincere glint. "I can certainly relate to that. Well, Miss…how rude of me, I have quite forgotten the formality of introductions. I do have the habit of getting straight to the heart of a matter."

"Forth. Maeve Forth," she supplied.

"Well, Miss Forth, I think it's safe to say that you have secured a position here at the Bates Library of International Studies."

She felt her shoulders immediately sag in relief. "Thank you, Sir."

"Sebastian," he supplied. "You can call me Sebastian."

So, her suspicions had been correct. This was the infamous Sebastian Bates. The sole heir to the Bates fortune. He stood and came around the desk. She stood as well, sliding the newspaper back into her satchel. He was a fairly tall man; his chin hovered just over the top of her head. Briefly, he touched her shoulder to guide her toward the exit and she felt a rush of warmth slide down her arm.

At the door he paused. "Report here first thing tomorrow morning and Marco will be the one to show you around. He's a nice guy and knows the ins and outs of everything."

Unsure if she would have the opportunity to see Sebastian again any time soon, she turned and looked over her shoulder at him. She wanted to impress upon him just how much this opportunity meant to her. How his simple gesture of hiring her for this position was life changing. The difference between a life of dependence and independence. "Thank you again, Sir—Sebastian. This opportunity truly does mean the world to me."

He bowed slightly in acknowledgement, a lock of black hair boyishly falling across his unwrinkled forehead. "It's my pleasure, Miss Forth. I am a busy man, but our paths will cross again; of that I have no doubt."

And with that she saw herself out.

2101
PARIS, FRANCE

The next morning, they left Le Temps.

Maeve had stayed up continually feeding the fire to keep the small attic warm. By the time they had fallen asleep, the pub below had grown silent. But Maeve was too keyed up to sleep. She kept playing her interaction with Sebastian over and over in her head.

He had been happy to see her. He knew who she was and what she was doing—altering his timeline—and he was still happy to see her. And despite what her brain kept telling her about the things she knew that he would do in the future, she had been happy to see him. Oh, when she saw him give his victory speech, she had felt afraid, but when he had kissed her on the street it felt for a brief moment as though nothing had changed between them. Except everything had. How could she love him when she knew what he would someday become?

One of the first questions the agency posits to new recruits is: If you could travel back into time, would you kill baby Hitler? The worst, most evil man in Pre-World War III history. It poses an interesting moral dilemma. First, not many people would be willing to kill an innocent baby. So there was that. That argument also brought in the entire debate of nature versus nurture. Surely, Hitler was not simply born with the desire to commit genocide in his DNA. Second, going back in time and killing someone before their actual death date, would have unforeseen ripple effects across all timelines of every person and nation in the world. A seemingly random person with a minute interaction could have a vastly different outcome, let alone significant people in that particular timeline.

Therefore, the agency didn't go back in time and kill individuals prematurely, but created subtle shifts, or as they called them nudges, that when added together over a longer period of time, created the desired change. Unfortunately, it was a lot of work and even with time travel, a time-consuming and complex process.

Time travel. Adolf Hitler and the Nazis had been fascinated with the idea of time travel. Die Glocke, was a bell that used some unknown radioactive element as a propulsion system to alter the spacetime continuum. Few people knew the SS was actually successful in this endeavor and that when the Axis Powers fell at the end of World War Two the technology was hidden away by the Allied Powers. Later after careful study, it was learned that the key ingredient was called Xerum 525, now commercially called Murex and used in the very device Maeve wore on her wrist.

Murex was like a radioactive mercury and scientists soon discovered after World War Three that the substance could be crystallized and used in a device as small as a watch to induce time travel. It was still considered a classified government technology though.

Thus, the agency, otherwise known as Operation Khonsu. Khonsu was the Egyptian god of the moon and associated with the passage of time because of the moon cycles. His name translates to traveler as he would travel across the night sky. Maeve often wondered if the Egyptians had the ability to time travel and that so-called modern humans were just too dumb to figure it out.

Maeve felt the truck come to a stop. She had finally fallen into a light sleep, and even though Elaina elbowed her in the ribs, she was already awake as soon as the prolonged movement of the vehicle ceased.

That morning in the cover of darkness, the three agents had snuck into the bed of a truck that was delivering barrels of ale at the pub's backdoor. A protective canvas was constructed over it giving them coverage and since all the barrels had been removed, it was rather comfortable going. She hadn't realized she'd fallen asleep.

Marco, who had been peeking out near the gate of the truck, turned his head and motioned for them to come. Maeve removed her satchel from beneath her head and scrambled to the edge of the truck bed. She could hear the driver speaking in loud French to someone near the driver's side of the truck. If they stuck to the passenger side it was unlikely they would be seen. The sun wasn't even all the way up yet.

When she slipped out letting the canvas drop behind her, Marco had already disappeared into an alley between two buildings. From the smell of it, they were near a bakery. The scent of baking bread made Maeve's stomach growl. They hadn't eaten breakfast and their paltry dinner hadn't been enough to tide her over.

Elaina crept up after them on feet like a cat. And Marco continued down the alley, northward toward the main thoroughfare. They looked like three people down on their luck looking for the odd job to make ends meet. Maeve had been sad to see the bundle containing their beautiful gowns drop into the Seine, but she was fairly certain Marco had not minded letting the butler uniform go.

This was where they would part ways for now.

It was her last chance to tell her team that Sebastian had recognized her.

As they reached the end of the alley, they stopped. They would exit separately onto the thoroughfare as opposed to as a group. Elaina went first. Before she exited onto the street, she winked at them and was gone—sucked up into the rush of people on the busy street.

Now that it was just the two of them—the two they'd been before Elaina had joined their team—she saw Marco's shoulders visibly relax. He always felt an odd responsibility for Elaina—Maeve wasn't sure if it was because of the girl's younger age or because of her carelessness or both.

"You know you aren't responsible for her, right?" she said softly. It was unlikely they'd be overheard with the din of the street traffic but she still whispered.

"She's just so young. It's hard not to be."

He stepped out of the alley and she followed him, falling into step beside him. She had tucked her dark hair up into her hat and wearing the boy's clothing, at a glance she could pass for a young man. Just two men walking down the street looking for work was not all that unusual.

"It's funny. I don't remember being as confident as Elaina when I was her age."

Marco shrugged. "She had a different upbringing."

That was true. Elaina also had a birthing mother but instead of being sent off to a boarding school, as a newborn she had been adopted right away by a wealthy couple who owned a minerals and ore mining enterprise. She was given the opportunity to become an agent not because she had been observed and subsequently cultivated, but because of her parents' government connections. Maeve suspected they hoped that formalized training would help to tame Elaina's free spirit which seemed to run roughshod over everything and everyone.

They walked along the now crowded street headed to the train station. They had one more stop before they could head home.

The snow had stopped and while it was still chilly, the sky was a clear blue. In the distance, the reconstruction of the Eiffel Tower stood sentry over the city. The Third War had a strange effect on technology. Most countries were thrown back a couple of centuries, before the rampant digitization of everything. Since the grid was one of the first things destroyed and if people wanted to survive, they had to go back to the old ways of doing things: growing food, transportation, heating and cooling, buildings were all now reminiscent of the old turn of the century architectural style. No more cement, glass and steel. It was certainly more aesthetically pleasing. Maeve still found it difficult to believe that people had flown in giant busses with wings in the sky and received money out of machines built into a wall whenever they wanted.

A horse pulling a carriage rattled past splashing dirty slush up onto the sidewalk. The world was an odd mixture of animal and machine. Not many people had cars because gasoline was scarce since the oil and gas pipelines had also been among the first things destroyed at the start of the war, but they had also been some of the first things repaired over the last several decades. Still, it was slow-going and as a commodity it was expensive.

"So, are you going to tell me what it was that you didn't want Elaina to know?" Marco gave her a sly smile. His hat was jauntily tilted covering one eye as he glanced at her. Her silence prodded him to add, "I know that he recognized you. But I also know that there's more."

Marco was one of the most intelligent people she knew and one of the best agents. She had been his protégé when she started out. He was only a year or two older than her, but he had started out much younger—when he was barely even a teenager—because of his savant level comprehension of physics and quantum mechanics. He was also a talented and accomplished pianist.

They were an excellent team because very rarely did they need to communicate with words. Unlike Elaina who had to constantly communicate with words and couldn't use silence as a means of expression. Maeve automatically rolled her eyes as the thought crossed her mind. That was also why Elaina did not accompany them on all their missions; only the level two ones.

So she was not surprised that Marco had noticed Sebastian's noticing.

"I should have known that he would," Maeve said truthfully. She was still uncertain if she wanted to tell him the entirety of it.

Marco let out a snort of laughter. "He couldn't take his eyes off you. Be honest, Maeve, in that emerald green dress you were kind of hard to miss, even in that shadowy alcove."

She sighed. "I'm going to miss that dress! It's a shame we had to throw it into the river."

"You're avoiding my point."

An old woman resembling a pile of dirty rags jostled a cup in front of them and Marco immediately dropped in a few coins, but they didn't stop walking.

"It was unnerving," Maeve said. "It has been nearly a decade since he's seen me last."

"Yes, but it's only been a few months for you."

Suddenly, she felt her throat constrict and the familiar sting of tears. Marco stopped and pulled her into the entrance of a tailor and fabric shop with the closed sign still turned.

He placed his hands on her shoulders. "Tell me what happened. Why were you late?"

There really was no hiding from Marco. She brushed a stray tear away. "He caught me outside, just before I was about to cross the street."

Marco's intense grip on her shoulders relaxed slightly. She continued, "Marco, he knew exactly why I was there. And he didn't even try to stop me! He-he kissed me and said he looked forward to seeing me again."

"He's a twisted man, Maeve. Well, not yet he's not. But he soon will be." He removed his hands and ran them through his brown hair. "It's like it's all just a game to him."

Except Maeve knew that wasn't true. It wasn't a game to Sebastian. Oh, sure, what was to come was some kind of demented game to him. They were still making alterations to the timeline in order to figure out just what caused Sebastian to turn from a wealthy man bent on achieving power to a sadistic overlord bent on creating a perfect utopian world. What and where was the pivot point to cause one of the most successful men in the new era to forfeit his soul? That was the Opus Mission.

When Maeve saw bits of the future, it was like watching a complete stranger, not the man she had once loved so deeply and intimately. The man that after their little encounter, she realized she still loved very much. That was the part she had to keep a secret, not just from Marco, but from herself as well.

2101
JUST OUTSIDE GENEVA, SWITZERLAND

The train ride was uneventful.

It was a good opportunity to sleep without fear of discovery. The little compartment had two bunk beds with curtains and while it was a fairly hard surface and the term bed was used rather loosely, it was not as hard as the attic floor at Le Temps and Maeve found that as soon as she pulled the curtain closed, she was asleep.

Her dreams flitted between her memories, like a bird darting between the trees of a forest. The feeling when Sebastian recognized her during his speech—that briefest of moments when his sapphire eyes locked on hers. The warm familiarity of his lips against hers, the golden light of the gaslit streetlamps falling across the hard lines of his face and the snow melting on her cheeks. Back in time to the first time that she had ever met him, sitting behind that gigantic mahogany desk in his office at the Bates Library of International Studies. Then the memories flitted to slightly more recent times like the last time that they had been together before their paths so abruptly diverged. She woke up with tears sliding down her face.

In the train car before they disembarked, Marco had snagged a suitcase from an unsuspecting couple. He'd shoved a few bills for their troubles into the man's coat pocket while they slept in a compartment in the next sleeping car over. Now he pulled out a garishly printed sweater, women's slacks and golden earrings for Maeve and a man's cable knit sweater and twill slacks for himself. The woman's sweater was too big for her, but once she put her coat back on, it wasn't noticeable and more importantly, it was warm. The slacks were also too long, but her boots were heeled which helped. Still the hem dragged on the ground. Marco's clothes fit him much better—it always seemed he had a much easier time finding suitable disguises that needed little to no alteration.

There was a small sink, fresh towels and little bars of soap in their compartment. They took turns scrubbing the soot and grime from their faces. The woman had a hairbrush in the suitcase, and Maeve gratefully stroked through the tangles in her own hair. When she was done her dark locks fell to her shoulders, nicely complementing the cream sweater even if it did have ugly abstract flowers on it. Marco combed some water through his hair, slicking it back off his forehead. He slipped the suitcase into the overhead compartment with their disregarded street urchin disguises. Now they looked like any other respectable couple and Maeve was glad to be dressed like a woman again. Even though she was considered a Level-3 agent, she still found it difficult to remember to deepen her voice and alter her gait so that she appeared more masculine when disguised as a boy. Often, she just forewent talking completely unless she was alone with Marco or asked a direct question by a stranger.

Geneva was even colder than Paris. When they disembarked, it was nearly dusk and the street lanterns were lit. The town had not been as hard hit during the war as other areas, but it still had suffered the repercussions of the nuclear fallout. Older trees grew in strange, gnarled patterns contrasted against trees that had been planted in more recent decades. The snow-capped mountains formed an imposing barrier in the distance, colored purple against the night sky.

Maeve looped her arm through Marco's as they walked down the sidewalk along the lake where the Rhône River fed into it. It was a weeknight, but there were still plenty of people out dining, shopping and enjoying the general ambience of a town coming alive again.

Marco put his hand over hers as they made their way to a stone building that had a turret capped with a copper roof, patinaed to a pale turquoise. The building had once stood magnificently with multi-colored stained-glass scenes of Jesus's birth, death and resurrection and of saints and angels, but now the windows were boarded up and the once tall spire with the little cross at the top was the only clear indication of what the building had once been. Wide steps led to a set of iron doors, but Marco led Maeve right past the church and through a small wrought-iron garden gate that led to what once had been the church's cemetery.

It was still a cemetery, but without a proper caretaker, headstones were tumbled over, some so deteriorated that they had crumbled away completely. Ivy had taken over much of the graveyard and was working its way over the flat stones once buried in the earth. Maeve suppressed a chill thinking about the bodies that were buried beneath her feet—bodies that had been buried in this spot hundreds of years ago and long before the war. Bones of the dead that had no idea of the atrocities that had been committed by those that still lived.

They exited out the other side of the cemetery in a twin of the gate through which they had entered. Around the back of the building was a stone archway that led to a set of stairs. Marco nudged her ahead of him and she clasped his hand instead of the railing as she made her way down the narrow steps. There was no light in the stairwell, save for the moon above and the door at the bottom had been propped open with an empty brown jug.

Marco pressed behind her as she peered into the narrow opening. There was a long hallway and at the end of it she could see a light. She nodded and Marco pulled the door open just enough for them both to squeeze in one after the other.

The hallway was made of limestone like the outside of the church. Now that they were inside and the soft din of the city had faded away, they could hear the murmur of voices.

Side by side they hurried down the hallway following the general direction of the voices. The hallway ended with a wooden crucifix nailed into the wall, someone had tied a red ribbon to it and the ribbon's ends were unraveling and tattered. On the floor beneath it were scattered papers and small coins and pieces of jewelry. Evidence of people still practicing the Old Religion even though it was now forbidden in many parts of the world.

The nuclear annihilation of World War Three was enough for some people to believe there was no God or that he had forsaken them, but for others the survival of a remnant of humanity and the slow repopulation of the planet was proof enough that God was sovereign over all things.

The glow of light and voices emanated from the left. When they looked to the right there was another set of steps that would lead up and into the main parts of the church above. The voices were where they needed to go.

There was no need to hide or sneak for this gathering. When they entered the open door, Maeve noticed there were about twenty people already in the dimly lit room. People sat in chairs that had been arranged in a circle or leaned against the perimeter walls speaking quietly to one another. Against one wall a folding table had been set up with some paper cups and a carafe of what smelled like coffee. No one looked up when they entered. The room was full of strangers.

All of these people were other agents. Not all of them working for the United States government, but various governments from around the world. There were hundreds of agents all over the world not just in the US agency. Some agents worked solo, and others worked in teams, but certainly there was no universal way to recognize one another on the street. However, that wasn't to say that there were not several ways of leaving signs or tokens to inform another agent of your presence.

The Opus Mission was the master mission, but it was filled with smaller, complex missions that more than any one team could handle. Periodically, they'd receive the coordinates for a gathering usually when something significant happened in the present or the future. The previous morning while they were getting ready to leave Le Temps, Maeve had noticed that she and Marco had received coordinates, but Elaina had not. Instead, the young girl was probably already back in the states debriefing the intelligence she had gathered while attending the victory party.

Reconnaissance was logged, catalogued and input into a massive database driven by artificial intelligence that then used various algorithms to generate different probabilities based on the inputs. While some technology from before the war had been reset, other tech had been kept strictly for the government's use. It had been carefully preserved and protected in an underground bunker inside of Mount Shasta in California. Artificial intelligence was one of those technologies (and time travel, naturally). When she was a Level One agent, Maeve's first assignment had been training the AI about Sebastian Bates.

In unspoken coordination, each agent moved to take a seat in the circle of chairs. An older woman with thick, silver-streaked black hair and somewhat severe eyebrows looked at her watch and moved to the center of the circle. She gave a nod, and an older gentleman wearing what looked like priestly vestments gently closed the door to the room. The windows of the room were high up and since it was night, the only light came from several lit sconces along the walls. It cast the people sitting in the circle in strange shadows. Maeve had dropped her arm from Marco's when they'd entered the room, but now he casually placed his arm across the back of her chair. Maeve noted the move for what it was: these people may be other agents, but that didn't mean that Marco trusted them.

"I will not mince words, folks," the woman began. They didn't introduce themselves at these meetings; just as they showed up at staggered, designated times, just as they would leave, there remained a certain level of anonymity. As a general rule of thumb, the less one knew, the less one could tell. That was also why no single person knew all of the information regarding the mission. And, why each agent didn't know too much personal information about other agents. It could be used against them if they were captured and compromise not only the agent's life but possibly the entire mission.

"We've received reliable intelligence that there was an assassination attempt on the Opposition Party candidate."

There was a tittering of shocked murmurs at this statement.

"In what year?" asked a man wearing a dark coat and hat with a red scarf that was still wrapped around his neck despite the relative warmth of the room.

"Present. Today at a rally in rural Oklahoma."

Geneva was seven hours ahead of Oklahoma. If it was dusk in Geneva, that meant it was likely still afternoon in Oklahoma and that the attempt had occurred in the morning.

"Does he live?" asked another voice standing in the shadows. It sounded like a woman.

"That's what we need to find out before chaos breaks out in the streets. You will receive messages from your respective agencies shortly. Unfortunately, that's all I have."

The room broke out in whispered conversation as the woman exited the circle and joined the priest near the coffee table. In a matter of seconds, timepieces around the room began to light up.

Maeve's lit up at the same time as Marco's.

He looked up at her after reading it and she nodded. She could read those brown eyes as easily as he could read her own. Standing, he took her hand in his and pulled her toward the door, nodding curtly at the older woman and the priest, who both acknowledged him in return.

Once they were in the hallway Marco picked up the pace and Maeve had to walk double-time to keep up with his long stride. He pulled her past the way they had come and instead of turning, went up the steps leading into the church above.

There was only a heavy velvet curtain at the top of the stairs. As Marco moved it dust puffed into the air and Maeve suppressed a sneeze. They came out near the pulpit, a large stone altar that stood abandoned and looked out on worn, wooden pews. Anything of value would have been stolen long ago. It was a miracle even any of this had survived. It was cold compared to the room below and Maeve could feel a draft coming in from around the boarded-up windows. Snow lined the edges of the floor. It was also dark. Besides the few outlines of the objects she'd already noted, there was little else she could see.

Without speaking, Marco released her hand and raised a finger to his timepiece. Maeve mimicked the motion. The date, time, and pinned coordinates had already been set. Along with the coordinates the message had simply read: *He will live. Find out how.*

"See you in Oklahoma," Marco said and activated his timepiece.

2091
NEW YORK CITY, UNITED STATES

Maeve sat in a small office that was approximately the size of a broom closet. She was trying to figure out just how the desk and chair in front of her even fit into the space. They surely hadn't come in through the door that was now behind her.

There were papers all over the desk, some spread out, some in haphazard piles. A gaslit sconce on the wall near the door provided little in the way of illumination. There were no windows because, as already observed, it was a closet. Stacks of books littered the floor creating little winding towers and a narrow path of bare floor wound its way from the door to the desk. Maeve was perched precariously on top one of these book piles because save for the single chair that Marco now sat in, there was no other. There was no room.

However, there was a file cabinet under the desk because currently Marco was rattling around inside one of the drawers.

"I know it's in here somewhere…"

She wondered if this room was considered a fire hazard.

"Ah, here it is!" He pulled out a dirty folder and grinned triumphantly at her. "New hire orientation!" He blew a bunch of dust off the file sending particles circulating into the air which was already quite stuffy. Maeve suppressed a sneeze. Marco didn't seem to notice. "It's been a while since we've hired someone."

That was good, right? Low employee turnover?

He pulled open the file which contained…a single piece of paper with scrawled handwriting across it. He considered it, a lock of brown hair falling across his forehead which he immediately pushed back by running his hand through his hair causing it to stick out in random angles.

Grimacing, he shoved the paper back into the folder.

"You know what? Let's just start with a tour of the library."

Maeve put her pen and notebook into her leather satchel which she still wore strapped across her body so that the small pouch landed at her hip.

"Yes, that's an excellent idea," he said. Although she wasn't sure if the comment was directed toward her or toward himself, so she just smiled encouragingly.

She suspected that Marco had no idea what he was doing. He was only a couple of years older than her, and he seemed intelligent, if not a wee bit disorganized. He stood and made his way through the piles of books.

They exited the broom closet—er, office—and emerged back into the main hallway. They were on the lower level of the building, beneath the street level where patrons entered and where Maeve had met Marco for the first time the afternoon prior.

The library really was quite massive. The lower level was like a labyrinth of hallways and rooms. They turned left and Marco walked to the end of the hallway where there was an arched entrance leading into a dark, unlit room. He reached for the lantern located on a hook on the wall inside the doorway and turned the switch to ignite the oil and it burst into life. The hallway had sconces periodically lit, but there was no point in wasting oil to burn lanterns in rooms not regularly in use.

He held up the lantern so it's light spilled farther out and she could see better. There was row after row of completely filled bookcases and a long table stacked with binders and more books running down the center of the room. The table bowed under the weight of the books.

"These are some of the donated books. We receive hundreds of donations a year from wealthy patrons all over the world—thus, the tagline International Studies. Since the library's inception, we've cataloged at least a million books, but donations still pour in. Some of them had been kept vaulted in private collections during the war; others have been carefully transcribed from fragile texts kept in museums and rebound into new editions for re-introduction to the public. Regardless of how they arrived here, these are just some of the books that still need catalogued and put into circulation upstairs."

Some of the books. Well, she certainly had her work cut out for her. There would be many long hours spent in this room in her very near future. Possibly later this afternoon.

Marco hung the lantern back on the hook by the door as they exited.

"In addition to cataloging those books, Mr. Bates thought there was another task to which you'd be well-suited." He led her down the hallway to a set of wide stairs.

It was a relatively short staircase, but it led to a floor with small windows—a half-floor in between the lower level and street level. There were small cubby-like spaces along the windows complete with various writing instruments, sheafs of paper, magnifying glasses and even white pairs of cotton gloves. Each space had its own lantern and chair as well. The ceiling was low but the morning light filtered in brightly through the line of windows. On the opposite wall was what looked like a walk-in vault of some kind with a large spinning dial on its door. Was this where they kept special books or reading material? The idea intrigued her.

She'd been fairly quiet that morning, both taking it all in and trying to appear amiable to her new boss. Well, one of her new bosses. Mr. Bates—Sebastian—was also her boss. This opportunity was too good to be true and she hadn't wanted to spoil it by potentially saying the wrong thing until she felt out Marco's personality a bit more.

However, upon seeing this room she couldn't help herself. "What is this place?"

Marco smiled and this was the first time since their second meeting that he seemed to visibly relax. "This is the Scribe Room."

He led her to the vault. There was a small window in the door and if she stood on tiptoe she could peer inside. The first door opened onto a small vestibule. There were hooks on the wall with white puffy fabric suits hanging. Beyond the vestibule she could see into the main chamber. All three walls were filled with books from floor to ceiling and in the center stood a long, narrow work table and a single chair.

"It looks like a vault, but what is it really?" she asked lowering back down.

"It's called the Immaculate Chamber, or I.C. for short. It's essentially a clean chamber. No natural light can get in and further deteriorate the fragile pages of the books or their bindings and no dust particles either. Scribes put on the clean suit and gloves before entering the chamber. Some of the books are simply too fragile to be exposed to even air, they would disintegrate, but they still need scribed and put into reprint."

There was the sound of footsteps behind them and Maeve turned to see Sebastian standing in the archway to the room. The natural light from the windows reflected off his shiny, jet-black hair which waved gracefully back from his forehead. Today he wore a gray suit and silver tie and waistcoat. The gray made his normally sapphirine eyes take on a stormy glint.

"I see you've found the Immaculate Chamber. Quite a feat, isn't she?" he asked. Before either of them could answer, he continued. "Marco, I just need to steal Maeve here for a few moments. I promise I'll return her to you shortly so that you can finish your tour."

A strange look briefly crossed Marco's features but he smiled and nodded. "Yes, Sir."

As they exited, when Maeve reached Sebastian, he held out his elbow and she looped her arm through his feeling an odd tingling sensation as she did so.

"I didn't realize you were so passionate about preservation, Mr. Bates. That chamber is amazing."

"Sebastian," he corrected. "And yes, my father was also quite passionate about restoring old manuscripts—he was keen to think of the Bates Library as a sort of modern Library of Alexandria." He led her down the hallway until they reached a small alcove with a metal gate. A small metal room was behind the gate and she realized this was a dumbwaiter to take them to other levels of the building.

Sebastian pulled the gate aside and gestured her into the metal box.

"You're familiar with the Library of Alexandria?"

"Certainly," she replied as he stepped in beside her and closed the gate. "Cleopatra herself studied there and it was one of the more interesting structures from the Hellenistic Ptolemaic era of Egyptian history. It's truly a shame that it was burned down and all that knowledge lost forever."

"Or was it?" Sebastian looked down at her and smiled mischievously. As he did so the metal room jostled and began to move. Startled she grabbed his forearm and he placed a warm hand over hers. "It takes a moment to get used to and, unfortunately, it isn't the smoothest of rides, but it does get the job done."

They creaked upward. Clanks and bangs echoed around them and Maeve felt certain at any moment the contraption that pulled them up through the building would stop and they'd go crashing back to the lower level. She didn't let go of Sebastian's arm and he didn't seem to mind.

It was difficult to hold a conversation over the obnoxious rattling noise of the dumbwaiter, so Maeve just watched in astonishment through the gate as the thick stone floors passed by them. The building was thirteen stories. Each floor provided a view of row after row and bookcase after bookcase filled top to bottom with books. She saw people browsing through the aisles, some reading in overstuffed chairs near the windows for the best light. Others she saw seated at tables with stacks of books beside them, scribbling in notebooks. Preservation was only a small portion of what the Bates Library of International Studies offered the citizens of New York. As far as she knew, there was nothing else yet like it in the entire world and for a moment she felt astonished that she was able to be a part of something so monumental and instrumental to the rebuilding of the world that had been destroyed so caustically due to power and greed.

So lost in thought was she that she didn't realize that the dumbwaiter had come to a stop.

"Penny for your thoughts?" Sebastian asked as he gently removed her hand from his arm and used both of his hands to pull aside the gate.

Feeling more confident now that they were stopped, she walked through the gate back onto the secure stone surface of the floor.

"I was just appreciating the magnitude of what you have created here. Your modern-day Library of Alexandria," she smiled at him as she once again looped her arm through his and felt that faint tingle.

The dumbwaiter had stopped on a room that took up the entire top level of the building. The ceiling was high and vaulted. There were windows that must have been ten feet tall and daylight streamed in. There was only one wall of bookcases on this level, but it was floor to ceiling with a ladder attached to a track. There were overstuffed chairs and luxurious oriental rugs on the floor. Eclectic finds were scattered about the room including a bust of who she recognized as the Greek philosopher Socrates. A giant fireplace of exquisite stone stood to one side and above it hung a painting of what she knew to be the Library of Alexandria, standing in all its glory on the shore of the Mediterranean Sea.

Sebastian smiled. "Welcome to my private reading area." He gestured toward one of the inviting chairs flanking the fireplace and she noticed there was a table set with a coffee pot, sugar, cream and two oversized cups. Was this standard procedure for a new employee's first day? She highly doubted that, but she was undoubtedly intrigued. Her teachers had always warned her that one day her curiosity would get the better of her, but Maeve had yet to encounter that day.

She sat.

He poured her a cup of coffee adding in cream until it turned a caramel color and handed it to her. He remembered how she took her coffee from the previous day.

The early morning light streamed into the room, softening the lines of Sebastian's face as he poured his own cup of coffee before taking the seat across from her. He was quite handsome in a devil may care debonair sort of way. How old was he? Mave wondered. Maybe a decade older than she? Thirty? He had spoken of his father in the past tense, so he was a wealthy, young bachelor. Educated, cultured, worldly even.

"What are you thinking?" he asked breaking into her thoughts. She hadn't realized that as much as she was conducting a study of him that he had been conducting a study of her. What she didn't realize at the time, was just how long he had been studying her. She decided to be forthright.

"About you. Educated, cultured—a lover of art and knowledge. Obviously, of great wealth. Handsome. I was wondering how it was that a woman hasn't yet captured your attention." She gestured to his hand holding the cup, which was ringless. She wasn't sure why she had answered so honestly. Something about Sebastian compelled her to truth.

He smiled and didn't interpret her observation as anything more than what it was. "I could say I am a busy man and have no time for such frivolities, but since you were truthful with me, I shall be truthful with you, Maeve. There hasn't been a woman who has captured my attention—yet."

She felt that odd sensation of tingling heat when he said the word yet. She changed the subject.

"Your taste in art is quite eclectic, Mr. Bates."

"Sebastian," he corrected again. "And as our dear friend Marcus Aurelius has pointed out: There is no nature which is inferior to art, for the arts imitate the nature of things."

"Is art how you study human nature?" she asked.

He set down his cup and stood. He began pacing across the oriental rug. She had the impression that a man like Sebastian wasn't good at sitting still. Men of action rarely were.

He stopped in front of the mantel, his back toward her as he stared at the painting above. It was quite a lovely painting. The white stone of the library and its copper dome with the sun glinting off. The turquoise water that seemed to leap to life off the canvas. In the foreground stood the Lighthouse at Alexandria, one of the original seven wonders of the world burning brightly and continuously, a beacon to the knowledge that saturated the shores of Alexandria.

"One of the ways. Paintings, sculptures, books."

He turned back toward her. His expression had lost some of its playfulness and his sapphire eyes had taken on a serious glint, the stormy gray specks returning.

"Well, you certainly have plenty of those things," she replied gesturing to the room in general.

"I've stolen you away from Marco this morning because I have a proposition for you."

She set her cup back down on the marble topped table between the two chairs.

"Sebastian, I am not…"

He chuckled deeply. "Not that kind of proposition."

She flushed but was visibly relieved. "What then?"

He began pacing again, head bowed and hands clasped behind his back. "When I met you yesterday, I knew instantly that you were the one who could help me. You see, I'd dreamed about you before you showed up. Needless to say, it was quite miraculous to see you appear here in the flesh, standing beside young Marco, eyes bright and shoulders back, ready to secure the position you had already clearly decided was yours for the taking."

He was rambling and it seemed contradictory to his nature. *Was he nervous?*

"I have been struggling with a certain text. A very, very old rare text. It's difficult to translate in its current condition. I need someone with the patience to scribe it to make the translation easier."

"Surely, you have staff better qualified than I? I have never done this before, as you know."

He looked up at her shaking his head. "No, no. That's just it. I want someone without the outside influence, who can scribe and help me translate with an unplagued mind. It's of the utmost importance. I would say I prayed for assistance, but we both can probably agree I am perhaps a bit pagan in my beliefs. Regardless, after I sought assistance from the powers that be, I had a dream of a beautiful young woman coming to my door. She wore an emerald green dress and had long dark hair and hazel eyes that were lit from within as if by an internal fire. Imagine my surprise when she showed up the next day asking for a position."

Maeve was dumbfounded. One, that he had referred to her as beautiful and two, that he was admitting all of this to her in the first place. He seemed too practical to put stake in a dream. "I wasn't wearing a green dress yesterday," she pointed out matter-of-factly.

He laughed. "No, you were not. But it was you all the same." He looked at her thoughtfully. "The green was very becoming though."

She felt heat rise up her neck. "What is this old, rare text? May I see it?"

He moved over to the bust of Socrates as if he were going to study it. Then just as quickly moved away again to resume pacing. She turned in her seat to follow him with her eyes.

"The provenance is not pristine, you see. At some point, it disappeared from the market for at least a century."

"The market? Is it considered an antiquity?"

He looked up and smiled again. It really did change his entire countenance. "You are a bright creature. Yes, it has passed from dealer to owner back to dealer over the millennia. During the war it disappeared entirely. That's where the provenance gets a little murky. But a few years ago, it popped back up onto the market. It's claimed to have been written by a mystic who lived in a cave in the mountains of what is now Turkey, and was then called Anatolia."

Maeve's brow furrowed as realization dawned. "The Eastern Land. The beginnings of civilization."

He stepped toward her and knelt down, resting his clasped hands on one of his knees so that he was eye-level with her

"Yes, see, I knew that you would understand. So will you consent to help me?"

It was hard to resist. A mysterious text of somewhat unknown origins that had been sold time and again on the illicit antiquities market, remaining among private collectors for thousands of years. Why? What was in that text that it should remain in the hands of private collectors and not available to the public? Sebastian had to have spent a hefty sum to acquire it. And although it was strange he had dreamed she would come to help him, even that odd bit of happenstance was hard for her to resist.

Now the wealthiest man in the entire world was kneeling before her seeking her assistance in his intellectual pursuits. Her assistance! Not even knowing if she was qualified except that his dream assured him that she was. She had come seeking independence and a steady income to prevent herself from a life of some kind of domestic servitude and twenty-four hours later she was being offered what could be considered the opportunity of a lifetime. It was like something out of one of the novels she spent so much time reading!

Looking directly into those sapphire depths that implored her, she answered.

"Yes, Sebastian. I will help you."

2101
UNDISCLOSED RURAL TOWN, OKLAHOMA, UNITED STATES

The world was spinning when Maeve landed with a thud.

She took a deep breath and pushed to her hands and knees. After all this time it never got easier. The sensation of vertigo was disorienting and then the physical landings were always rough. It took her a minute to gather her bearings. The first few times she had vomited and the world had seemed like it was tilted on its axis. Marco had told her that she would eventually get used to it, and while he hadn't been wrong, he hadn't been exactly right either. Maeve suspected she would never get used to the bending of spacetime.

When she stood up and took an inventory of her surroundings she was in a grassy field. The sun was low in the sky. There wasn't snow on the ground, but she could see her breath in the air. There were some cows a little ways away staring at her curiously. She looked down—no cow pies and no mud, so that was a positive. In front of her was a worn wooden split-rail fence in need of repair; she climbed over it easily and stayed in the shadow of the tree line as she got the lay of the land.

To her left was the cow pasture and to her right was a large red barn. On its side was a faded triennial American flag. 2076 had been the three-hundred-year anniversary of the signing of the United States Declaration of Independence. It seemed even more significant since it fell only a handful of decades after the end of the Third World War.

She edged along the tree line making her way toward the barn. Nearly all the major American cities had been decimated by the nuclear blasts. Rural areas more than three-hundred miles from the impact sites had less effects from the nuclear fallout. It was like being thrown back to the early nineteenth century with an odd mix of late twentieth century and early twenty-first century thrown in.

A familiar male voice called her name. She turned and saw Marco step out of the tree line.

He hurried toward her and grabbed her hand, pulling her around the massive barn and toward a gravel driveway.

"I checked the directions. The town hall is this way. That's where we need to go. It's about a quarter mile from here."

She could hear horses in the barn and the mooing cows in the distance. There was a tractor and some other farm equipment she couldn't identify sitting along the driveway. Up the hill she could see a small blue house with a long front porch. They went the opposite way from the house, down and around various other pastures, one full of sheep busily eating at a trough.

"I've never been to a farm before," Maeve thought but she must have said it out loud because Marco pulled her closer.

"Sorry, but we don't have time for a tour," he replied.

"It's just so different than the city. Do you hear that?"

He stopped and looked down at her with a frown. "Hear what?"

"Nothing. There's no noise out here."

"Well, that's the country for you," Marco replied, resuming their pace and turning off the driveway and onto the road.

"Why would the Opposition Party hold a rally out here? It's in the middle of nowhere."

She could see the town center in the distance. It appeared that the road they were walking down was the main road running through town. They stayed close to the shoulder. No cars passed them. One side of the road was forest and the other was just open prairie that looked like it went on for miles and miles.

"That's exactly the reason why they hold a rally out here. Because it's the middle of nowhere. These are the people that care the most, Maeve, because they're impacted the most."

She knew he was right. If there was anything that she'd learned in the last few years, it was that the people who seemed to have the least were the ones who had the most to lose. All those ladies and gentlemen in their expensive evening attire, gowns and jewels, drinking champagne at the Victory Party. All those elite donors to Sebastian's political campaign. They didn't even have a clue what they were funding. Not yet anyways. She wondered if they knew, if they'd change their minds.

Unlikely, she thought. Power has an insatiable appetite.

They reached the edge of town.

Marco checked his watch and nodded.

"This way."

It was a quintessential American small town with rows of buildings on either side and well-kept sidewalks.

The town seemed deserted.

The shops were all closed with shades drawn or lights completely off. Only a lone beat-up looking pick-up truck that had seen better days sat by the curb.

"Where is everyone?" Maeve asked.

Somewhere in the distance, she could faintly hear the bark of a dog. The town was really just these thousand feet of street. She could see where it ended and the road continued on in the distance disappearing into the horizon. As a girl who had primarily grown up around the city, she found the lack of people astonishing. So far, they had encountered more animals than people.

Marco stopped at the last building on their right. It didn't appear to be open. There was a closed sign on the door and the blinds in the main window were drawn. The peeling gold paint on the glass indicated that this was a bar called Pop's Hops. Maeve stepped forward anyways and tried the handle even though she got the result that she had anticipated. Locked.

Farther down the sidewalk the row of buildings abruptly ended as did the sidewalk. They stepped off the curb and onto a mixture of dirt, gravel and grass. A faded mural to greet visitors of the small town was painted along the side of the building, mainly depicting the prairie and the setting sun. There were a few cows and a horse that strongly resembled a dog. Maeve wasn't sure if that was due to the fading or the skill of the artist.

They rounded the corner of the building. Here there were more cars—all older models that ran on gasoline or diesel—and even a couple of horses tied to a dilapidated fence post. Their ears pricked up at new visitors but their leads hung loose and they generally seemed disinterested.

There was a large dumpster that smelled like rotting food near the back door to the bar. There was a door nearby which probably led into a hallway or kitchen. Marco pulled on the metal handle and the steel door slowly opened. She edged closer behind him. They were greeted with a rush of cool air and the soft murmur of voices, but the space was dark.

Marco turned his head so that she could better hear him. "There's a hallway in front of us that I think leads to the front of the bar—what we would have seen from the sidewalk. It's dark that way, but to the right there's a set of stairs going down and I can see a faint light."

"Okay," she whispered back and leaned against him as he stepped forward. So that they were chest to back. She slowly let the heavy door close behind her, engulfing them in darkness.

Marco's night vision was like a cat and his hearing like that of an owl. It was one of the reasons why she knew she could trust him on these missions. He found her hand again and led her to the right and down the dark stairs. They stepped softly but she could tell the stairs were made of wood and from the smell of must that the walls were made of concrete or stone.

The murmur of voices swelled and subsided. She could see the light now—just a faint glow cast from the left deeper into the basement.

They reached the bottom and Marco paused. Maeve felt something brush against her leg and suppressed the urge to scream. It had been trained out of her. Agents did not scream out—especially in unknown, potentially dangerous situations.

"Just a cat," Marco said softly. She let out the breath she had been holding. She must have squeezed Marco's hand without realizing when the cat brushed up against her. When she looked down, she could see that the cat had moved to the second from the bottom step and was watching them with curious yellow eyes.

Marco moved them into the space at the bottom of the steps. As her eyes finally began to adjust, Maeve could see that it was lined with shelves that were filled with various goods. From crates of jars and cans to sacks full of dry goods. In the room beyond the storage area was where the light was emanating from.

Silently they made their way across and to the door which was ajar, explaining why it had been so difficult to hear the voices or see the light from within the room beyond.

At the door Marco paused to listen. He gave a nod and he slowly widened the door opening so they could slip inside. The cat pushed past them and further opened the door. The light was coming from a single lantern hanging on a hook over the center of the room—it created only a small circle of illumination so that the edges of the room were thrown into darkness.

The people stood clustered around the center of the room and Maeve could see that there was a small wooden stage with a stool on it.

Marco let go of her hand and immediately disappeared into the shadows. She stayed by the door, slipping back into the dimness. The cat sat at her feet still watching her curiously, its tail swishing softly. As long as he didn't start making a racket that drew attention to her location, she'd take the cat's presence as a reassurance.

She stayed close to the wall so she could keep both the makeshift stage and the door in her peripheral view.

A hush fell over the murmuring crowd as a man stepped out from behind a curtain that was at the back of the stage. There must be another room beyond this one. She wondered how many of the above ground shops were connected through this maze of a basement.

Once he was all the way into the light, Maeve could see that the man was wearing a white lab coat smeared with dark stains and that he had a stethoscope hanging around his neck. His brown hair was sticking every which way, but he had long sideburns, a beard and a mustache. The overhead lantern light glinted off his glasses giving him a sinister look—like a mad scientist from Dr. Jekyll and Mr. Hyde. Upon closer study, the dark stains appeared to be blood. The crowd had grown so silent that you could have heard a pin drop. Even the cat had stopped swishing its tail and Maeve realized that she was holding her breath again—afraid to exhale and break the spell that had fallen over the room.

The man cleared his throat and croaked out two words. "He lives."

The simple statement caused the room to erupt into cheers. People were crying and hugging one another. And Maeve let out the breath that she had been holding.

Once the celebratory feeling died down—and what a contradictory celebration compared to the one whence she had just returned—the man continued to speak.

"However, I have bad news. The road will not be easy. And while he technically lives—"

A murmur broke out again and the mood in the room shifted. There was still the sense of relief, but now a sense of confusion permeated the initial reaction.

"What do you mean technically?" someone called out— oddly, it sounded like Marco. She had no idea where he was and the voice sounded like it came from above her and to the left. She glanced up into the darkness above and noticed there was row after row of low rafters. It would be just like Marco to climb up into the rafters to conduct his surveillance. She knew he was likely there and even she couldn't spot him.

The doctor cleared his throat again. "One bullet shot off the entire right side of his face."

The crowd gasped and Maeve did too. The agency believed the Opposition candidate was their only hope for a peaceful future. And for a chance at true prosperity.

"The other entered here." The doctor gestured at the upper left of his chest, indicating the region of his heart. "And the third, here." He indicated his lower abdomen. "The right eye is missing—but we have the left eye and the other surgeons—we believe it's enough."

Maeve's jaw had fallen open. No way. There was no way that they were going to be able to pull this off. What this doctor seemed to be suggesting; it hadn't been done—at least not successfully. It was a huge risk.

A woman came out from behind the curtain. She was wearing a red skirt suit and a cobalt blue blouse. She had an American flag pinned to her lapel. Her brown hair was cut in a blunt bob at her chin. Her red heels clicked across the makeshift stage and as she stepped into the light, it became clear that she was holding a stainless-steel tray.

On that tray was a what looked like a giant mason jar filled with some kind of liquid. The doctor picked up the jar with two hands and held it up toward the light overhead. When he did that, the people gasped again and Maeve could see that a single brown-irised eyeball removed from the socket was suspended in the liquid. She knew then that was all that remained of the Opposition Party candidate. A left eyeball.

"We will reconstruct Bartholemew Joseph Higgins from the cells in this single eyeball. It will be time consuming and will potentially take months, but it is enough. The Victory Party will not succeed in their attempts to destroy us—to destroy our spirits!" The doctor had hit his stride now. People were nodding in agreement and silently pumping their fists into the air.

Someone started up a chant. "Bart. Bart. Bart."

"We will have our candidate. And he will be stronger and better than ever before!"

Maeve had seen enough. As the crowd rallied, she edged back out of the room. Now that she knew the way, she found the stairs and silently hurried up them and out through the back door and into the coolness of the evening.

What the doctor was proposing was radical and risky.

Human cells had been regenerated in labs and then supplemented with 3-D parts to try and create a synthetic human. The results had been adequate at best. Even with a brain implanted and injected with human memories—essentially a microchip—there lacked a certain, well, *humanness* to the experiment. As far as Maeve knew there was no way to harness the essence of a human being—their soul as some would call it—and manufacture it. She was all for science—it was the very reason that she was even born in the first place. But these Neo-Science experiments encroached dangerously on the boundary between human and anti-human.

When Marco emerged, she was waiting at the hitching post, petting the nose of one of the horses. She said good-bye to the mare and fell in step beside Marco as they headed down the road and farther out of the town.

It was twilight even though it was still early evening and the sky was a deep violet gray.

After a long stretch of silence as they both pondered what they'd just witnessed, Maeve finally asked, "Did you notice anything from the vantage point of the rafters?"

"I should have known you'd recognize my voice."

"A decade working together will do that."

"I could see a little bit behind that curtain and into the next room. There were several doctors and I assume scientists gathered around a table. I couldn't see much, but I could hazard a guess."

"Do you think they'll be successful?"

Marco was quiet for nearly a full minute. "I think they have more motivation than ever before to get it right. And quickly."

"But it won't truly be Bart. They say he lives. But that won't be him. A person isn't a person if they have no soul, Marco."

"Unless…"

"Unless…" she echoed. They stopped walking and were facing one another in the dirt road. He took both of her hands in his and she knew exactly what he was thinking before he even said anything.

"It's just a myth, Marco."

"Sebastian thought it was important. Important enough to hire the valedictorian out of the Hartford School for Ladies, who just so happened to stumble into the only library in the continental US for a job one day. Who was then secreted away to start translating a highly controversial text…"

"But even Sebastian agreed that it was only a myth."

"A myth about how to preserve the soul of a person. It seems a strange coincidence, doesn't it? What exactly did Sebastian say, Maeve? *Remember.*"

His brown eyes were intense and he squeezed her hands a bit harder as if by doing so he could force the memory to reappear in her mind's eye from sheer force of his will.

"He said…"

Piercing blue eyes and lips curved in an easy smile with a hint of playfulness filled her vision. He had leaned over her shoulder as she explained a particularly interesting piece of the translation to him—he'd always loved their debates about history, literature, and theology. Both of them had; those arguments had been the catalyst for their relationship.

It may be a myth, Maeve Darling, but all myths carry an element of truth.

2091
NEW YORK CITY, UNITED STATES

The oil lanterns burned brightly and a fire burned low in the fire place.

Maeve paced back and forth chewing on the end of a pen. A ghastly, unladylike habit. But when she was thinking deeply or trying to solve a particular problem, the urge to move was irresistible. She was barefoot and the oriental rug between her toes was soft and plush underfoot. The fire was warm and emitted a soft glow.

So lost in thought was she that she didn't even notice when the door creaked open and closed.

"You're still here?"

Sebastian stepped into his personal reading room, shrugging out of his suit jacket as he did so. He tossed it unceremoniously onto a low upholstered bench near the door.

"Hmmm?" Maeve responded absent-mindedly.

He stepped closer and gently grabbed her elbow, jarring her out of her reverie. She looked around as if startled. Noticing the darkness outside the windows and the pinpricks of stars across the sky, she turned into his touch.

"What time is it? It must be so late! I lost track of all sense of time."

"Seven. Have you eaten?"

Seven! Her hand absently went to her cheek. She must look a mess. Her hair was pinned up with a pencil and fell in tendrils around her face. She considered his question. Indeed, she had not eaten since lunch. Truly she had lost all sense of time. The ancient text he had asked for her help translating—deciphering was more like it—had captured her mind almost instantly. It was all she could think about for the last month. Outside of her other duties at the library, of course.

He took hold of both of her forearms and guided her toward one of the upholstered chairs that flanked the fireplace. He found one of her boots kicked under the chair she now sat in; the other was precariously close to the fireplace. Once he retrieved them, he gently took each foot in his large hands and slipped them into the boots and began tying them.

"Sebastian. Surely, that's not necessary. What are you doing?" she tried to swat his hands away from tying the laces, but he ignored her.

"I am taking you to dinner. This will not do. Hours spent dead to the outside world, in here translating. You need sustenance, my dear."

"Truly. It's not necessary. I can just go home…I had no idea how late the time had gotten."

He ignored her protests and presented her with the sweater she had haphazardly draped over the back of the other chair. She stood as he held it for her then picked up the suit jacket he'd only just discarded.

There was a small antique mirror on the mantle and she caught sight of herself. She was right. She was a fright. Taking down her hair from its makeshift chignon, she shook it out and the dark waves tumbled to her shoulders. Her cheeks were flushed from the pacing and the warmth of the fire. As she inspected herself, she saw Sebastian watching her in the reflection of the mirror. A small smile curved his lips.

Feeling more in the present, she grabbed her satchel and dropped both her notebook and her writing utensils inside. Indeed, she had been holed up in Sebastian's personal reading room—which he had offered for her extraneous services—for hours after her workday had officially ended.

He had given her full reign over the room. It had wonderful light and was shut away from the rest of the library. More importantly, nobody disturbed her because Sebastian only ever had expected visitors.

She really had commandeered the space. There was a small writing desk now covered with her looseleaf notes and the ancient text sat open on the top. Following her eyes, he moved from the door and picked up the text, placing a ribbon to mark her place before he closed it. He then went to one of the bookshelves, reached in, and pressed on the back of the bookcase. A small compartment popped open and he placed the text—which was relatively small; pocket-sized almost— into the carved-out space. He shut the compartment and rearranged a few books in front of it. It was on a shelf high enough that without the ladder, Maeve had to stand on tiptoe to reach it.

He scooped her arm in his hand as he led her out the door, pausing only to lock it behind them.

They took the dumbwaiter to the wide main staircase down to the lobby which was empty at this late hour. Even Marco had gone home long ago. It was dark, only a small lamp burned, but Sebastian knew the space as well as he knew his own face.

There was a more discreet single door off to the side of the library's main entrance, they went out this door, also locking it behind them. The main doors had already been locked hours ago.

The library may have been deserted but at this hour, the streets of New York were not. People bundled against the crisp fall air—that time of year where the days are still somewhat warm, but the nights have a chill to them—dashed about the sidewalks busily.

She had no idea where Sebastian was taking her. He'd never done anything like this before and the look on his face when she caught him watching her in the mirror had been strange. It wasn't an expression she'd ever seen on his countenance before.

He zigged and zagged through the city blocks with confident steps. She hadn't lived in New York City very long, but when she'd read in the newspaper about the Bates International Library, she knew deep in the very core of her being that it was where she was meant to be. Among the books and the literature—a place of infinite opportunity to grow, learn, and expand her mind.

When they reached a block lined with quaint shops and cafes, Sebastian finally slowed his pace. The lamp posts glowed warmly and it was a picturesque little block, which couldn't be said for every section of the city. Maeve had never been to this part of the city before.

A short way down the street, Sebastian ducked into a small restaurant with a green and white stripped awning above the door. A Matre'd was stationed at the entrance. He was an older man with a droopy brown mustache, bushy brown eyebrows, and stooped shoulders. To Maeve he resembled a very sad, furry sheep dog, but his face erupted into a grin when he saw Sebastian.

"Monsieur, Bates! Quelle pleasure!" His French accent was exquisite. He scrambled for two menus and led the way without further comment.

They wove through the little restaurant which was actually quite busy. The atmosphere was warm and inviting. Truth be told, she felt a little underdressed in her simple black sweater, slim ankle length trousers and little boots. Since her outfit was all varying shades of black, gray and charcoal she figured maybe she would just blend into the background. Ladies stopped and stared as they strode past. This was something to which Maeve had grown accustomed when she saw other women interact with Sebastian. Most women smiled appreciatively at his handsome and stately presence. A few babbled incessantly and a few others stuttered incoherently. Even fewer attempted to flirt with him which often died rather quickly with a curt remark from Sebastian who seemed quite unaware of his own attractiveness.

"Here we are, Monsieur." The stooped man, who once he was straightened was actually rather tall, presented them to a quiet table in a corner near the front window. There was a little vignette of three candles burning on a hammered brass tray set on the table, decorated with white roses and white peonies.

"*Merci, Simon.* Your best Pinot Noir vintage, if you'd be so good." He pronounced Simon *see-mon.*

"Oui, *certainement*, Monsieur Bates." Simon bowed slightly and disappeared.

"You come here often, I presume?" Maeve smiled as Sebastian pulled out her chair before seating himself.

"A time or two." His smile belied his lie. "If you don't mind, I'd like to order for you. I know all the best dishes here. No special allergies or preferences?"

"None whatsoever."

"Excellent. You won't be disappointed."

When Simon returned, he had brought two chilled glasses and a bottle of wine in a bucket of ice. He popped the cork and graciously poured. As he presented the glasses to Sebastian, the latter told him: "The usual Simon, but par deux, *s'il vous plait.*"

"Excellent, Monsieur. I will inform the kitchen *immédiatement.*" He bowed once more and set off toward a set of swinging doors on the back wall.

"He's an efficient, fellow," Maeve smiled taking a sip of her wine. It was spicy and dry with a hint of fruit.

"Simon is a recent French immigrant. France has been a bit slow to rebuild shall we say, and he sensed an opportunity to re-establish himself and his family here in New York. He's a wonderful man. And a hard worker," he added.

Sebastian swirled the liquid in his glass and took a long inhale from it before taking a sip. Evidently, he was a connoisseur of wine just as he was with literature. She wondered what experiences had made him so cultured and worldly. He was incredibly wealthy—one of the wealthiest of America's Nouveau Rich Post-World War III. The families that had invested in seeding and repopulating plants, animals, and people are the same ones that fared off immediately. The earth needed to be re-established and infrastructure recreated. There was money to be made around the things that people needed to rebuild, and people needed food and shelter. Despite the horrors of the past, the cycle continues and the world carries on.

"Thank you for this." She gestured to encompass the small restaurant.

"Nonsense. You have to eat as do I, so I figured why not do it together. A little extra treat is that I actually enjoy your company."

This statement surprised her.

"You don't enjoy the company of others?"

He conceded. "Not many."

She took another sip of wine, careful not to over indulge before dinner was brought to them. Now that she was here and smelling the aroma of fresh baked bread, stewing tomatoes, and various spices her stomach clenched with hunger. How silly she had been to allow herself to get so lost in her work that she had forgotten all sense of time!

Sebastian mistook her silence for want of an explanation.

"I have a difficult time, how do the young ones say it, making friends? I am a busy man, which many supposed friends don't seem to appreciate or understand, except of course my business colleagues. What free time I do have, I don't want to spend with someone frivolous."

As if to emphasize his latter statement a high-pitched giggle filled the restaurant.

A few tables over was a pleasant enough looking man with tawny hair combed over into a neat swoop and beside him sat a young woman whose blonde hair was piled high up onto her head. It sparkled with diamond pins that caught the light. The amount of makeup she wore made her seem older than she likely was as it caked in the creases of her face and her dress was too low cut to be considered decent. She was laughing and fluttering her eyelashes foolishly at something the man had clearly said. His face flushed with either embarrassment or pleasure; Maeve found that it was hard to tell.

Sebastian glanced over at the couple then his sapphirine eyes came back and fell on Maeve. She certainly had never been accused of being frivolous. Too sensible, practical to a fault, bookish, boring, overly educated too independent…these were some of the words that had been used by others to describe her. Most of them said when they thought that she couldn't hear. Unfortunately, a small handful of people were not shy about sharing these things to her face.

Nervous under this new found scrutiny, she brought up the only topic she knew that could shift the attention away from herself: work.

"Well, the Liber Vitae is certainly anything but frivolous," she offered.

Sebastian took another sip of wine. "That is a truer statement than ever said before. It's a little-known text. So many have spent millennia obsessed with the Book of Death in its various iterations. But why obsess with death when you can instead obsess over life?"

Maeve smiled. "I would argue that people are obsessed with death because it's the quintessential unknown. Whereas with life, we all know what life entails as we live it every day."

Sebastian grinned. He enjoyed their little debates as much as she did.

"It is not death that a man should fear, but he should fear never beginning to live." He quoted Marcus Aurelius.

"Touché," Maeve conceded.

At that moment a waiter brought out a large tray covered with various dishes. He laid them out across the table: a basket with chunks of baguette, white fish in a tomato sauce, long green beans with slivered almonds, and a platter of various cheeses garnished with green olives.

Sebastian waved his hand in the air as if to clear it of their previous discussion. "Enough talk of work; let us talk about something more interesting."

Maeve took a bite of warm baguette and swallowed. "Such as?"

He grinned. "You."

In the back of her mind, she had suspected this moment would arise. They had been working together for over a month now and until this moment, the relationship had been strictly professional. She'd gone out to the pub with Marco after work a couple of times and had gotten to know him a bit more casually, quickly considering him a friend she could count on and keep as reliable counsel in a city where she knew very few—if any—people. Marco was intelligent, funny and kind. Sebastian was still somewhat of an enigma. Even Marco admitted that after working at the library for several years, he still knew very little about his boss except that he was one of the wealthiest men in the nation and an astute businessman with a passionate love of culture, art, and history.

Maeve had been able to chip away at the hard shell little by little. Maybe only a hairline fracture. She knew that Sebastian loved rare artifacts and antiquities and would attend undisclosed private auctions to purchase obscure texts—such as the Liber Vitae. She also knew that he could fluently speak at least half a dozen languages: French, Italian, German, Spanish, Portuguese, and Greek. And those were only the ones that she had overheard and could identify.

"What could you possibly want to know that you don't already know?"

"Truly, I only know the basics of your upbringing and education, but what interests me more than your humble beginnings, is that spark I see in you. *Je ne sais quoi.* For a woman of a simple, almost ordinary background, you have an ambition and intellect few other women have that I have known."

She took a bite of fish and chewed thoughtfully before responding. "I suppose it was my birthing mother. She was a woman of African ancestry and I have fragmented early memories of stories—legends and myths of her people. But I was too young—a baby really—to understand. But I loved the sound of her voice. The way it undulated as she told a story. When I got sent away to school, one of my first teachers was kind enough to notice how curious I was and instead of squashing it, she encouraged it. She began to give me books to read. Books from friends or any that she could find really. It started me on a journey of insatiable curiosity. The world is so vast. History so convoluted. There is much to learn."

"Your teacher was a wise woman," he replied.

"And a great woman full of honor and duty."

"And your birthing mother? Is she still alive?"

Maeve shook her head. "Sadly, no. I was told later that I was her last birth."

A birthing mother over a lifetime, typically only had ten births. Not all babies were raised by their birthing mothers, but since Maeve had been the last, her mother had decided to raise her until she was school-aged, practically still a toddler. By then the woman was well into her fifties. If she'd still been alive, she'd have been close to ninety years old.

Sebastian took a thoughtful sip of wine. "I'm sorry to hear that. I'd have liked to thank her for the wonderful job she did impressing wonder upon you."

The meal continued with amiable conversation and as the time passed, Maeve could feel herself relax more. Sebastian was as curious as she and witty to boot. It was a side of him she didn't often see although she could sense it lurking beneath the carefully curated façade. He didn't always smile easily, but when he did it reached his eyes and they sparkled like the gems of their namesake. He was an incredibly handsome and intelligent man and she was thankful for this opportunity to get to know him better. Men like Sebastian could certainly help to open doors, especially in a society that viewed women with renewed skepticism.

After Sebastian personally thanked the chef and kitchen staff, tipping everyone generously and bidding a fond farewell to Simon, they left the small restaurant with full stomachs and happy hearts.

It was definitely late now and Sebastian offered to walk her home. Home was only a few blocks away. The air had grown cooler and her thin sweater was not enough to keep the chill away. Noticing her shivering, Sebastian removed his suit jacket and placed it over her shoulders, then placed a causal arm around her waist as they walked. She didn't mind. Not one bit.

The walk passed quickly and before she knew it, they were standing at the entrance to her little rented townhouse. It was a plain looking red brick building with white trim and a cheerful green front door. It was in a part of town that was a mix of students and working-class people. But she was friendly with all her neighbors and there was a sweet little floral shop right next door.

She unlocked the door and paused unsure of what to do.

But Sebastian, ever the gentleman, made the decision for her.

"Thank you for the wonderful company this evening, Maeve."

Before she could hazard a reply, he quickly brushed his lips across her cheek and disappeared down the steps and back into the night. She let herself inside the door, closing and locking it behind her. He'd left so quickly; she realized that she was still wearing his suit jacket. The now familiar smell of earthy cologne and faint cigar smoke filled her nostrils. She'd return it to him tomorrow, but for now she was going to bask in the glow of a memorable evening she wouldn't soon forget.

2,000 BC
ANATOLIA (MODERN DAY TURKEY)

The ancient wisdom had to be shared. For centuries it had been passed down from high priest to high priest.

Now a young high priest with more modern sensibilities had decided that the ancient traditions should be recorded in written hand. He packed a light repast of bread and cheese into his satchel, strapped on an animal skin of water, and gathered up an as-yet unused clay tablet and his reed stylus.

He didn't take a donkey but chose to walk the miles long trek to the high mountain. The high mountain was revered because the people believed the higher that one could get on the earthly plane, the closer they would be to God.

His leather sandals slapped against the rockface as he walked. The sun shone brightly and the sky was cloudless and blue. A gentle breeze came through the canyon as he made his way toward the high mountain. Some of the other high priests ridiculed him. They did not think his idea to record their most ancient wisdom was a good one, but the young high priest knew that the younger generation would not believe without a written record. A written record would provide structure and instruction in their ways, he had argued. Written word could not be taken out of context and manipulated as easily as the spoken word.

So, while he didn't have the blessing of all of his fellow priests, he knew in his heart that God was the one who had planted the seed in his mind and was now guiding him. When he reached the summit, he removed the colorful, woven shawl that had been around his shoulders and placed it on the ground before sitting. He carefully removed his tablet and stylus from his bag.

Before beginning he looked down and out across the valley and the varying shades of white, tan, and red sprinkled with green from the sparse shrubbery of the mountains. He revered the silence of the mountain. The high mountain brought one physically closer to God, but also the peaceful tranquility of the summit allowed one to hear God better, without the noise of the village below.

He closed his eyes and reached out to God for His guidance. A pleasant warm sensation moved through his body and he took it as one last confirmation that he was obeying the request from God to record the ancient wisdom. He didn't know how or why, but knew in his heart that someday this text would be written and re-written through time and preserved for future generations. The secret of the priesthood would be a secret no more. The ancient wisdom was meant for all to understand because God wanted all his children to be in awe of His glory.

The young priest smiled as he began to carefully create wedge marks in the soft clay, recording the word of God for all to come to know and understand.

2101
NEW YORK CITY, UNITED STATES

Maeve was not looking forward to their mission debriefing. Her mind was spinning with the things she had seen and heard in the last forty-eight hours.

Not to mention that time travel took its toll both mentally and physically. Sometimes in the form of headaches and nausea, but it always seemed that her body needed precious time to catch up and shake the lag.

She tried to gather her thoughts as she took a shower, allowing the hot water to pinken her skin and the steam to fill the bathroom. She did her best thinking in the shower.

First, there was Sebastian's victory. It had not been unexpected, but the support he received from the upper echelons of society was more troublesome than she had realized. They were unwittingly slow walking themselves to a fate for which even they were ill-prepared.

Then there was the assassination attempt on Barty, as he was affectionately known by his passionate followers. He was the Every Man Candidate. The one who represented the regular, working-class citizen. Bartholemew Jospeh Higgins was the one who for decades since the Third World War offered actionable hope to a population that had quickly realized the machinations that had led the world to its near annihilation were still at play. And the people were rising up to finally say: No More.

Who had committed the atrocity of attempted murder? Not just murder. Assassination. Maeve wondered if another team had been sent down that rabbit hole. The agency's work was precarious because it was a delicate process to create the subtle alterations of the past that would ultimately influence the future. The alterations were carefully studied and the "stitches" as they called them had to be both perfect and unnoticeable; otherwise, the results could be disastrous.

And then as if those two things weren't enough, there was the little consideration of what the Opposition Party surgeons and scientists planned to do. It was ironic that she had spent two years of her life translating the ancient text that it appeared they were going to use to resurrect Barty back from death. All they needed to recreate him was the tiniest bit of DNA, which they had been able to obtain in the surviving left eyeball. Then the ancient wisdom would take care of the rest.

The hot water pelted her head and she closed her eyes.

She hadn't realized then what she had been working on. Correction, she had known what it was she was working on; what she hadn't known was how her translation would potentially come to be used.

She recalled how Sebastian had presented her with the task and she wasn't even sure he had known or had understood the ramifications of translating that old text into modern language. A text that had been lost to humanity for millennia. And for what she now knew was good reason. There were just some things that humans were not meant to mess with.

And then last but not least, she thought as she got dressed, was that kiss. Her heart and body had responded instantly to Sebastian's touch, completely overriding her brain. It irritated her that he could still have that effect on her. She hadn't truly been surprised when he had recognized her; she would certainly recognize him—the heart knows what the mind cannot begin to understand. What had surprised her was that he cared enough to still pursue her after all this time.

Halfheartedly, she threw her hair up into a ponytail and grabbed her leather satchel. She plugged in the coordinates for headquarters and braced herself for the hit of nausea.

2101

MOUNT SHASTA, NORTHERN CALIFORNIA UNITED STATES

Headquarters, also known simply as HQ, for the secret governmental program known as Operation Khonsu was located in Mount Shasta. Not on, but inside the mountain itself.

Mount Shasta was an enigma to those interested in both the paranormal and in governmental conspiracies—a term that had fallen out of fashion once it became widely known that Project Mockingbird had been used by the CIA after the John

F. Kennedy assassination to deem anyone who questioned the legitimacy of the assassination's government narrative as a conspiracy theorist. It had taken over sixty years for that information to become declassified to the American public.

However, that then became the perfect opportunity for Project Echo. Project Echo worked under the same premise: the use of government propaganda that was disseminated to all the major news outlets in order to inform the public of appropriate narratives and to dismiss anyone who questioned those narratives. The American People had been duped once, surely their own government wouldn't have the chutzpah to dupe them again? Wrong. Trick me once, shame on you. Trick me twice, shame on me. Propaganda was the secret weapon of all modern world governments and how those in control could ensure that they remained in power. If you couldn't be certain of the truth, and you couldn't question the truth, then they would remain the sole arbitrators of truth. As one great American author had once said, *definitions belong to the definers not to the defined.*

Maeve made her way up the mountain path. It looked innocuous enough. From all appearances, there was no indication the mountain was anything except a mountain. The government had realized its past mistakes in announcing its presence with signs, fences, and security cameras in the past. That type of thing only made people more curious and more suspicious. Better to just blend in rather than blatantly announce one's presence.

She found the little crevice in the mountain side that was faux rock and pressed it. A small dark glass circle appeared and she swiped her watch face to her badge barcode to be scanned. It beeped its approval and the mountain seemed to shake as a ten-foot door slid open in front of her. She knew it was stainless steel coated with titanium and then modeled with a façade of faux stones to mimic the gray and tan striations of the mountain.

When she stepped inside the door immediately closed behind her. A tunnel lit with rows of dim light guided her path. In the present, this building was the only one that she'd ever been in that had decent electricity. But it wasn't connected to the grid; it used its own source of nuclear power.

The tunnel was made of steel and her footsteps echoed sharply all around her. It resonated to the right and to the left, up and down, created to disorient someone so that they didn't know exactly where they were inside the great mountain.

At the end of the tunnel was another steel door, this one with heavy rivets. This time the scanner was not disguised and she held up her badge to its lens. The doors opened without a sound.

Now she was in a large open space with the hum of voices coming from all directions. There was a sleek stainless steel and glass desk in front of her with multiple flat screen monitors across it. A middle-aged woman with brown hair streaked with gray strands sat behind the desk monitoring the screens. As soon as Maeve had broken through the electromagnetic field, the woman would have received a notification of her presence. The subsequent ID scans and facial recognition would have confirmed her identity before she'd even made it this far onto the premises.

"Welcome back, Maeve. Haven't seen you in a while."

"Hey, Martha," Maeve scanned her badge once more on the little scanner built into Martha's desk. Martha's tenure predated Maeve's arrival. She was a no-nonsense kind of woman, but Maeve found her to always be friendly and a straight shooter.

Martha lowered her voice and leaned toward Maeve. "The LT is freaking out a bit over these latest developments. I wouldn't get too comfortable being back on this timeline."

Maeve nodded. She'd expected as much. She only wondered if she'd be sent forward or backward in the timeline. "Well, it was good while it lasted. A hot shower in my own home is always a nice reprieve, no matter how brief."

Martha smiled understandingly and Maeve made her way to the elevators. It was always disconcerting coming here. The place seemed so futuristic and alien compared to the world outside. Inside HQ resembled a very sterile space ship. Everything was stainless steel, titanium and glass. The inside was an open shaft where the elevators ran up and down and the offices, meeting rooms and laboratories ran along the perimeter. The building had one hundred floors and while she had entered at what was considered ground level, she knew there were at least ten floors below that main level that went deep into the mountain's base. Down there were additional laboratories that she didn't have clearance to gain admittance or to even see.

The elevator stopped at the thirty-third floor and Maeve stepped out, turning right. Most of the offices and meeting rooms had glass walls and doors and she could see people taking phone calls, sitting at long tables debriefing or discussing various plans, and others furiously typing at computers.

Operation Khonsu was a large division of the HQ workforce, but there were also other governmental agencies located within the mountain. Some simply had a presence, like the NCIA—New Central Intelligence Agency after the old one had been disbanded for its role in World War Three—and others she didn't even know their names or acronyms. For the most part the various agencies behaved only within their individual silos.

In the past, governmental agencies working in conjunction with one another was one of the primary causes of the Third World War. Unbeknownst to the executive and legislative branches of government, various agencies had worked together along with various wealthy corporate executives to create a totalitarian system that bypassed the highest powers, working in tandem and in secret to lead the entire world straight into the biggest catastrophe since the Big Bang.

Rebuilding was slow and establishing trust again not only with the American population, but that of the rebirthing world, was even slower. Maeve's study of the events and dynamics leading up to the Third World War had led her to believe that the apprehension was warranted.

And here they were again unbeknownst to many, with a new technology on hand to help thwart the same kinds of things from happening all over again. History was useless if people refused to learn from it.

She reached the end of the row of meeting rooms and passed through a doorway leading to several rooms with drywall and no glass. One of the doors simply read Khonsu in black metal letters and that's the one Maeve pulled open.

The lobby was a small sterile room, but it did have a sleek countertop with a coffee pot and small white mugs with Shasta printed in block letters, packets of sugar, a kettle of hot water and various tea leaves and strainers. There were green glass bottles of water and small clear bottles of fresh cream perched invitingly inside a stainless-steel bowl of ice. The lobby also had a couple of upholstered chairs that had seen better days and were in stark contrast to the sleek modernity of the rest of the building.

As she made herself a cup of coffee she recalled when she had sat in one of those chairs nervously waiting for her interview. At the time, she'd had no idea how the agency had even found her. One day a cryptic typed letter had arrived at her townhouse instructing her to be at this location on the twelfth of April at noon if she was interested in learning about a new opportunity. She had thought it was weird at first and had ignored the summons. But as the date on the original letter came closer, she received more letters stating the same thing and the last one had contained a boarding pass for a train to Northern California. A train ride was a rare privilege because it was so expensive. Especially travelling from New York to California. Finally, curiosity had won out. It could have been dangerous, but what was life without at least a little risk?

Now she knew that the agency had found her through Marco.

Coffee in hand, she made her way down a short hallway and opened the door to the debriefing room. There were no windows in the entire building since it was located inside the mountain, but special lights that mimicked daylight were installed overhead to give the rooms a somewhat natural feel. As natural as fake could be anyways. A convincing faux fig plant stretched in the corner. At the end of the room opposite the door was a flat screen monitor mounted onto the wall. Marco and Elaina were both already there seated at the long rectangular table made out of some kind of old, glossy composite wood. The finish left fingerprints, spills and smudges and constantly needed polished.

Elaina started to say something, but their Lieutenant must have somehow sensed Maeve's arrival because the lights dimmed and the screen at the end of the table lit up. Maeve hurried to a seat next to Marco and across from Elaina.

The Lieutenant's face came into view. It was a face Maeve wasn't sure she'd ever get used to. She'd never met the Lieutenant in person. In fact, she didn't even know the Lieutenant's name. At the upper levels of the agency, secrecy was even more intense.

Lieutenant had frazzled gray hair that spread out around her head like a grizzled halo. Her eyes were small dark gray beads—well, the one that they could see—the other was covered by a black eye patch that no one asked about. Her mouth was small and puckered like a sour rose bud and her face had the folds of time. Dark eyebrows arched so high that the Lieutenant always appeared to have an inquiring expression even when she was not inquiring.

"Nice of you to join us, Forth," the gruff voice rattled.

Maeve resisted the urge to roll her eyes. She had not only been on time, but even a few minutes early. She did not regret the extra time she took in the hot shower that morning nor the exchange of pleasantries with Martha. Under the table Marco bumped his knee into hers in a playful acknowledgement and Elaina snickered because she was a brown noser.

In typical Lieutenant fashion, she cut right to the chase.

"I've read the reports you all have submitted and before I let you know your new assignments—yes, that's plural—I had a few questions." She glanced down at something then looked over at Marco. "Simmons, in your Paris report you stated that the servants and other staff seemed appreciative and jovial to be working with Bates. Can you elaborate?"

There were no mincing words with the Lieutenant, so Marco's answer was short and concise.

"They're well paid. Paying staff well makes them not only happy, but loyal."

Lieutenant nodded. "Quite." She looked down again. "In Oklahoma, you state in your report that the only viable physical remains of Higgins was his left eyeball."

"Correct."

Elaina's pretty face formed a pout as she realized that Maeve and Marco had been on a mission without her, but even she knew that as a level two agent, there were certain missions simply above her rank.

"Forth, your Oklahoma report corroborates with Simmons except that you added a note regarding the Resurrection Text."

It was a question formed as a statement.

Maeve shifted in her seat.

"While my note is purely speculation, I'd have been remiss not to mention it. The Libre Vitae would appear to be the only viable way for them to bring Barty back. All the scientists would need is a handful of live DNA cells, which they have in the remaining left eyeball. If they have that, then their statement is true that Barty lives, at least theoretically."

The Lieutenant didn't look happy about this news, but she grunted in agreement.

Just then both Marco and Elaina's timepieces lit up simultaneously. They looked down, then at one another and then at Maeve whose timepiece had remained dark.

"Simmons, Black, you're dismissed."

Elaina looked like she was about to protest—not only had she been left out of a mission, but she also hadn't been asked any questions about her report, and now apparently Maeve was going to get some kind of special treatment—but Marco shot her a look that made her mouth snap shut.

He squeezed Maeve's shoulder as he followed Elaina out of the small room and shut the door behind him.

Maeve swallowed nervously. This had never happened before and her mind automatically started going through the past couple of missions and the contents of her report to spot something that would require a reprimand, but she couldn't think of a single thing.

The Lieutenant looked down at her from the giant screen. The lights were still dim and now that she was all alone the Lieutenant's face took on a slightly more menacing countenance.

As she looked down at Maeve, Lieutenant tried to smile but it came across as more of a snarl. Maeve shrank back into her chair.

"Congratulations, Forth. You are about to embark on your first solo mission."

Startled by this revelation, all Maeve could manage was a timid, "Ma'am?"

"You're a level four agent now, Forth. Level fours are approved to take solo missions."

"Thank you," Maeve said uncertain of the proper response. She was getting a promotion for her work, so she assumed an expression of gratitude was more or less appropriate.

The Lieutenant cleared her throat.

"Your aptitude and ability to piece together otherwise seemingly irrelevant pieces of information makes you an especially interesting agent. You will meet up with Simmons and Black shortly, but first you need to take a trip to Egypt. The coordinates have been sent to you."

Maeve's watch face lit up. Cairo, Egypt 2079. The past then.

She looked back up at the screen. The Lieutenant continued.

"You are going to find Bates and see who he purchased the Libre Vitae from. Sources say it originated in Anatolia and that eventually it made its way to Egypt. We need to know how. And we need to know first how it fell into the hands of Sebastian Bates and second how the Opposition Party got hold of the information."

Realization dawned on Maeve just then: if the Opposition Party had access to the same information as what had been Sebastian's life work, then that could mean that there was a double agent in the party's midst.

The Lieutenant saw the realization dawn on Maeve's face. "You understand the importance of this mission. Good. And, uh, congratulations."

The screen went black before Maeve could respond and she was left sitting alone in the debriefing room as the lights came back up.

Her first solo mission.

2079
CAIRO, EGYPT

The air hit her like a ton of bricks when she landed. The smells of camel, donkey, spicy food and unwashed bodies did not mix well with the nausea induced from time travel.

She ducked behind some brambles and vomited up the toast she'd quickly eaten for breakfast. Wiping her mouth on her sleeve she rose, crouching down behind the brambles and careful not to step in her own vomit. Really the smell just coalesced with the overall ambience. This was not the first impression she thought she'd have of Egypt, a place that she had always dreamed of visiting.

First things first, she needed to get her bearings. Egypt hadn't been one of the areas as hard hit during the Third World

War. This timeline was some forty plus years past and the main players had been the United States, Russia, China, and Europe. Regions such as South America and Africa were less effected than other continents from the results of nuclear fallout.

She spotted a woman who looked like a European tourist and Maeve decided that was as good an identity as any to emulate. The fashions hadn't changed that much and her black trousers and cream shirtwaist would suffice for now. She rolled her sleeves up to the elbow and readjusted her satchel across her shoulder. An American tourist.

A line of camels being led with more tourists perched awkwardly on their backs passed by and Maeve used it as her opportunity to step out from behind the brambles. Her stomach still roiled slightly and she figured it would probably be a good idea to grab a cup of coffee and try a light bite to eat. Maybe it would help to settle her stomach. Besides, she needed to make a plan of how to find Sebastian so that she could follow him for a few days and learn his routines.

She scanned the area and spotted Shepheard's Hotel. From what she knew this was the third incarnation of the grand hotel. In 1952 the original structure, which had been quite the place to be seen in its heyday during the exciting discoveries in the latter part of the nineteenth century and earlier parts of the twentieth century, had been destroyed in the Great Cairo fire. By 1960 it had been rebuilt, much of the historical beauty lost to more modern design—at least on the outside. Then almost a century 'later it had suffered some destruction during the Third World War from Communist rebels, and this time when it was rebuilt, they had taken pains to restore it back to its nineteenth century glory.

Being a lover of history had certainly benefitted Maeve thus far as a time travel agent.

Vendors were selling various items as she approached the steps to the hotel's entrance. A variety of flowers, charms— whether authentic or replica only a knowing eye could tell— and sweet meats. Her stomach had settled as she grew accustomed to the mixture of smells that she figured was uniquely Cairo. A bustling city oasis in the middle of the desert.

She entered through the opulent lobby of Shepheard's and turned to her right where there was a dining area open to the public. She asked the host to seat her on the terrace that overlooked the street below.

The Egyptian air was dry and the sun was shining strongly. She ordered coffee, bacon, and a basket of various breakfast muffins. She needed to make that plan and wasn't sure how long it would take to come up with one that was actually feasible. The service was five-star and her just ordered breakfast appeared almost immediately before her. She nodded her thanks to the waiter and took a sip of coffee as she looked out across the Nile River.

It was always strange to her when she landed in these places where time seemed to have stood still while the rest of the world had exploded into chaos. Tourism had always been a mainstay of the Egyptian economy and even now it seemed to be flourishing once again. Dragomen gathered groups of men, women and children to load up on donkeys and camels to head toward the various pyramid and temple sites.

Quickly acclimated to the sights and sounds, Maeve took out a notebook. Knowing Sebastian as well as she thought she did, she was going to make a list of the types of places that she would be most likely to find him. He had obliquely mentioned several trips to Cairo and Luxor, but it was only a couple of the many cities around the world to which he'd traveled. One could not create an International Library by staying planted where one was.

The waiter returned to her table.

"For you, Sitt," he said in flawless English, but addressing her with the Arabic title.

He handed her a large bulging envelope and she thanked him.

Her name was scrawled across the front in an unfamiliar hand. Unsealing it she found a map of Cairo and a bundle of Egyptian pounds along with various identification papers in case she was detained. The papers included American, Egyptian, British, and French identities. There was also a receipt for a week's stay at the Shepheard Hotel, prepaid, and a small key with a room number engraved upon it. The agency was certainly thorough.

Is this what a solo mission was like? Because this she could certainly get used to.

She kept the map and shoved the rest of the envelope into her satchel and returned to her list.

Nibbling on a corn muffin, she pondered the places Sebastian was likely to visit. Antiquities dealers for sure. She knew that some of the shops that sold replicas had closed door deals that were only accessible by word of mouth or a recommendation from another patron. Sebastian's love of history and culture surely meant he would visit the various archaeological sites and the Cario Museum. Having finished the corn muffin, she chewed on the eraser of her pencil.

Those all seemed as good as any place to start. Finally, setting down her pencil and helping herself to another cup of coffee and a cranberry muffin, she examined the map. She could make her way to the Khan el-Khalili, a famous Egyptian *suk* or market. It was a longish walk from the hotel, but it would also allow her to stop at the new National Museum on her way.

Sitting back in her chair she finished her bacon and coffee. Overall, she was satisfied with the plan. Her first solo mission and a promotion! She was now the same level agent as Marco. She wondered if he knew. She also wondered when it was that she would see him (and Elaina) again. What mission had they been sent on before she was told about her new status?

Leaving a few bills on the table, she stood up and stretched. It would be nice sleeping in an actual bed for once and having access to a shower. She could even stop and pick up a few clothing articles. Yes, indeed, she could certainly get used to this.

Satiated and not wanting to waste the expanse of day still before her, she made her way down the terrace steps and through the little gated entrance that led her back onto the main street. She'd have to walk farther into the city and into the downtown area in order to reach the market.

A variety of voices speaking English and Arabic flowed around her as she crossed the main street, avoiding camels, horses, donkey, carriages and the occasional car. It was a bright warm day. Shops had their doors open to welcome visitors and it felt good to be in a place that was warm and inviting instead of the usual cold and sterile places she ended up in.

The Third World War had started over forty years prior and was over almost as soon as it had begun thanks to the use of nuclear weapons. It had started innocuously enough, or so she had learned, with the planned release of bio-engineered contagions that allowed for quick shifts of money, power, and control. Tensions around the world had increased and small wars—could a war ever be called small? —broke out between various countries. Many of the larger countries engaged in proxy wars using smaller countries as pawns, uncaring of civilian casualties and against many civilian wishes for peace and stability.

Once the people had experienced several years of violent turmoil, on top of the turmoil already suffered during the years of socially engineered pandemics, citizens all around the world had risen up in revolt against their governments. They had had enough of manipulation, destruction, and death. They expected more from their governments. But they were not to get it. Rebel pockets broke out in cities all over the globe and as their numbers increased and some countries aligned with the rebels, the bigger countries that held all the power felt it slipping through their fingers. There was one way to silence the people. And it was a way from which many of the regular, working citizens didn't have adequate protection. Regular people did not have million-dollar bunkers to hide away in. If the blasts didn't kill them, the radiation from nuclear fall-out would surely do so and did. The rebels would be annihilated and the most powerful could then rebuild the world to suit their needs and desires.

As she walked, she continued to notice that this little forgotten part of the world seemed to have been inoculated from the worst of it. In the early years of the war, there was mass migration. Many people had fled the larger, more populous countries seeking refuge in smaller countries more concerned with preservation than self-annihilation. Afterward, the entire world had been thrown back in time and it was more of a crawl than a climb back to normalcy. And while it was said that to some degree no part of the Earth had been left untouched by World War Three, there were some blissful pockets that Maeve would occasionally stumble upon that seemed to have avoided the brunt of it. This place was one of them.

The Nile shone brilliantly and the sun was warm on her head and shoulders. She ducked into a small shop that appeared to be a combination of a tailor and a milliner and purchased a wide-brimmed straw hat adorned with a white silk ribbon. There was no reason that she shouldn't avoid sunburn on this mission.

As she made her way closer to the city center more shops had their doors thrown open with their wares tumbling out. She stopped and perused a table of *ubshetis* and small amulets that would have been used to protect the dead. Another shop had a table of pyramids and obelisks made out of various stones and gems and of all shapes and sizes. Another shop sold handmade leather sandals, bags, and belts.

Her senses had quickly adjusted to the sights, sounds, and smells. A cacophony of languages and accents rang out coalesced with the gentle snapping of sails as boats made their way down the Nile. With the brim of her hat casting her face in shadow, she realized it was the first time in a long time she'd felt anonymous.

She reached the new National Museum which looked more like a palace than any museum she had ever seen. Its limestone façade was broken up by forty-six human-sized key-hole shaped windows and in its center a pair of giant, wooden double doors.

Upon entering, she paid the fee and turned down a guided tour in order to wander at her leisure. She picked up a map and examined it. The museum seemed to be a mixture of art and history. She had always wanted to see artifacts from the exhumation of King Tut's tomb. Unfortunately, his mummy was in situ in Luxor and a visit there wasn't currently on her agenda.

Her boots clicked against the white marble floors as she made her way back to the New Kingdom exhibit. King Tut was an 18th dynasty pharaoh in the mid-1300s. He was the son of the heretic pharaoh Akhenaten who changed the state religion from a polytheistic one to a monotheistic one, centered around the sun god Aten. In later years, much of the history of his reign was eradicated.

Two ornate hieroglyphic-covered obelisks at least twenty feet tall stood sentry on either side of the New Kingdom room. From her studies, she knew that some obelisks like the one created by Hatshepsut were nearly 93 feet tall. A feat she could scarcely comprehend. Stepping over the room's threshold, Maeve's breath was nearly taken away by the beauty. The walls were covered from floor to ceiling in vibrantly colored frescoes depicting various scenes of daily Egyptian life. Long glass cases held various artifacts with plaques providing descriptions; many of the discoveries occurring in the late nineteenth and early twentieth centuries.

But the real show stopper was the ceiling. Which was painted a rich cerulean blue with yellow stars that reminded Maeve of a starfish. A replica of the ceiling of Queen Nefertari's tomb. There must have been hundreds of hand-painted stars on the arched ceiling above her head, and with the light filtering in from those massive windows the feeling was almost ethereal. Standing in the middle of the room with her head thrown back, mouth slightly agape, for just a brief moment she felt as if she had been transported back in time.

There were limits to time travel. She could not go back to the Eighteenth Egyptian Dynasty for a little firsthand visit. The agency's time travel was all mission centered and closely monitored. It was not a technology widely known nor used outside of government capacity. Technically, it was considered a classified technology and it would likely be a long time before it was declassified.

Still, she felt in that brief moment the awe that must have been felt upon the discovery of that tomb in 1904.

"Magnificent, isn't it?"

She hadn't heard anyone else step into the room, but she turned at the familiar voice. A young man in his early twenties stood beside her. He had wavy black hair and a short and tidy beard. His shirt sleeves were rolled up to the elbow revealing strong, tanned forearms and his collar was unbuttoned exposing his tanned neck and revealing a jade green faience crocodile head amulet thread through with leather cord. He was dressed for outdoor work with heavy boots caked in dried dirt.

He was looking at the ceiling when he addressed her and now he looked down at her, his sapphire blue eyes bright with curiosity. *Well, that had been almost too easy,* she thought.

"Magnificent is an understatement. I don't think there are words to describe it," she replied truthfully.

"You should see the real thing," he said. His smile revealed perfect white teeth.

"Unfortunately, the Valley of the Queen isn't on my itinerary for this visit."

"Well, that's a darn shame. But this truly is a magnificent replica. It was painted by hand and took ten artisans over a thousand hours to create."

"You're a fan of Egyptian art and history?"

He smiled again. "Something like that."

She didn't want to lose him as soon as she'd found him. She was about half a dozen years his senior now; this was his youth when he had traveled the world collecting books and art for his international library before he'd settled back down in the states and before he became his father's sole heir.

She stuck out her hand and hoped he wouldn't notice the slight tremor from nerves.

"You seem to know a lot. I'd love a little tour from someone with your expertise, that is if you have the time. My name is Maeve."

He took her hand in his rough, calloused one. His eyes matched the color of the ceiling above their heads and sparkled not with stars, but what was clearly mischief.

"Oh, I have the time. You can call me Seb. It's short for Sebastian, but no one around here calls me that."

***

She didn't know what luck had allowed for her to so easily find Sebastian. Maybe it wasn't luck at all, but fate. They were always drawn together like two magnets. And as the afternoon wore on, she found herself quickly falling in love with this version of the man as well. He was smart, articulate, and charming.

He had taken her around the New Kingdom exhibit, explaining the various artifacts to her—what they were, what they were used for, and when they had been discovered and by whom. He pointed out the nuances of the painted frescoes and could read the hieroglyphics without consulting a book or interpretation guide.

They went from the New Kingdom to the Old Kingdom and Maeve found herself lost in Sebastian's narration of the five-hundred years that constituted the Old Kingdom's reign. They had spent a good amount of time in front of one particular scene that depicted the weighing of the heart of the deceased against the feather of Ma'at, the Egyptian goddess of truth and justice. If the heart, or soul, was too burdened and heavy with sin, then the deceased would not find the paradise that awaited him when he died.

The afternoon had passed by in a blur of art, history and Sebastian regaling her with the stories of old.

Now they sat at a small café with a lovely view of the Nile and the setting sun illuminating it in a golden wash of color. Plates of hummus, unleavened bread, and skewers of lamb and beef filled their table. She had not said no when Sebastian ordered a bottle of white wine which they now sipped leisurely as they enjoyed their meal.

In her recent past, she had fallen in love with Sebastian the business man and scholar, but this was the Sebastian that had laid the groundwork for the one she had fallen in love with so easily over many late nights and intellectual debates. This was Sebastian the collector—the collector of art and history, but more importantly of stories.

As they sat looking out over the river watching the ships sail by, he said, "I'd love to open a library someday. Make all of this knowledge of history and culture and art available to anyone and everyone."

"So much was lost during the war," she agreed taking a sip of her wine. Her spine prickled at his prophetic statement.

He turned and looked at her, his sapphirine eyes sad. "Not just lost, Maeve. But forgotten."

She wished that she could tell him his desire would come to fruition and that he would open the Bates Library for International Studies and painstakingly spend hours translating and scribing badly damaged texts so that he could bring back what was once lost.

She also wished that she could simply enjoy this moment, but she also knew that she had a mission to do and prolonging the inevitable would only make her job that much more difficult. She'd delayed as much as she could even without anticipating that she would be able to find Sebastian so quickly. She needed to find out how he had acquired the Libre Vitae. Actually, she needed to first find out if he had even acquired it yet at this exact point in time.

He had been very knowledgeable about the ceremony of the weighing of the heart explaining to her how it was important to the Egyptians to lead a life of truth and justice. According to the Book of the Dead, an individual's heart revealed their character and their actions during their life. The jackal-headed god Anubis oversaw the ceremony and the ibis-headed god Thoth recorded the results. If the heart was equal to the feather of Ma'at then the individual was allowed to pass on into the afterlife, or paradise. If it was heavier, a chimera that had the head of a crocodile, the forequarters of a lion, and the hindquarters of a hippopotamus would devour the individual.

"The moniker of the god Ammit was the 'devourer of the dead.' It's interesting that in New Kingdom texts Ammit had a more central role and although he was a god, he was more akin to a demon than a deity," Sebastian explained.

"What about in the Old Kingdom?" she asked taking another sip of her wine. The sun now hung low in the sky casting the world in dusky shades of lavender, mauve and blue as stars began to appear in the sky above the city. She couldn't think of a recent time that had felt more magical with possibility than this moment.

Seb—as she was getting used to thinking of him—grinned. "In the Old Kingdom, Ammit was less prevalent. The god Khonsu, the god of the moon, was instead depicted as the 'devourer of the dead and hearts' in ancient texts. In what's referred to as Spell 310 in the Book of the Dead, Khonsu burned the hearts that failed the test of truth and in the subsequent spell, he devoured the hearts of the gods and the dead. The hearts of the gods contained much power."

Maeve's skin prickled at the mention of her agency's name. She had known Khonsu was the god of the moon and the phases of the moon were a means of tracking cyclic time, but she had not known this other element of the agency's namesake. For a second, she had the briefest sensation of foreboding—until a ship's horn sounded in the distance and the sensation fled.

Seb continued, "The hearts of the dead that failed judgment were devoured and left the individual trapped in the Egyptian equivalent of hell, called Duat."

"What the Romans and Greeks would refer to as the Underworld."

"Exactly."

He poured the last of the bottle of wine into his glass and swirled it before taking a sip. The gesture transported Maeve to a night many years in the past for her, but many years in the future for Sebastian.

"When was the Book of the Dead found?" she asked breaking the spell that had briefly fallen over her.

"An actual book of bound texts from beginning to end was never found if that's what you're asking. In the nineteenth century, various papyri were found and collected that had the sole theme of an individual's journey into the afterlife and contained various spells and ceremonies."

She sensed her opening.

"If there's a Book of the Dead, is there also a Book of Life?"

She stared out at the river watching a dahabeeyah pass by with its passengers leaning over the rails and the white sails flapping in the breeze. She felt more than saw Seb's intense gaze fall on her.

"I think you know the answer to that," he said.

When she turned, he was staring at her with blazing bright eyes. His lips were quirked up at the corners and he leaned back in his chair sipping his wine.

"Do I?" she asked.

He took out a silver case and took his time lighting a cigarette before answering her.

"You're a smart woman. Was it an accident that you were at the museum today when I happened to be there examining the papyri of the Book of the Dead in the archival room?"

She ignored the implication. "You have access to the archive room? What were you searching for?"

He tilted his head. "A clue."

"And did you find it?" she asked.

He set down his glass. "Actually, I did."

"But you still haven't answered my question. Is there a Book of Life?"

His gaze swooped back out toward the Nile before swinging back toward her. "The Libre Vitae. You never answered *my* question. Was it an accident?"

He put out his cigarette.

She had the advantage of knowing Sebastian very well and knew the best strategy was to equivocate. "It was serendipity." At least that wasn't a complete lie.

He threw back his head and laughed—the sound was both comforting and familiar to her ears. His smile was wide as he picked up his glass and drained it before jumping up to his feet. He extended his hand across the table.

"Come with me."

"Now? Where are we going?"

"Do you trust me?" He was looking down at her, sapphire orbs alight and smile mischievous. A lock of black hair fell across his forehead. This Sebastian was young and daring. Less cautious than the man she knew. But it was still the same man. She stood placing her hand in his.

She did not lie when she replied. "With my life."

2091
NEW YORK CITY, UNITED STATES

Books were continually being delivered to the Bates Library for International Studies.

Boxes and crates from all over the world arrived daily. Some of them were donated from wealthy collectors, others were ones Sebastian had come across in his travels and had shipped back to New York. Every day more and more deliveries arrived. They were carted via the dumbwaiter down into the fifth subfloor where they were stored before being unpacked, categorized and catalogued.

This was where Maeve found Marco one morning about two weeks after her enchanting dinner with Sebastian. She had scarcely seen him since then because the following day he'd flown out to Egypt to meet with one of his antiquities dealers and then was headed to Greece for a business meeting with a potential donor for the library. He wasn't set to return for a couple of more days.

Marco's sleeves were pushed up to his elbows and his hands were on his hips. His brown hair stuck out every which way and Maeve knew that meant he had been running his hands through it repeatedly as he contemplated something. He was standing among several stacks of crates that were nearly as tall as he was.

"There you are! It's about time!" he said in exasperation looking at the odd timepiece he wore. It was a bit flashy for what she considered Marco's character, but when she had commented on it, he had shrugged her off by saying that it was a family heirloom.

"I'm not late," she replied ignoring the unwarranted remarks. She was in fact on-time just as she was every day. "Another shipment?"

"Yes, this one is from Egypt. I swear it's more work for us when he travels than when he's here."

"But it's good, isn't it? All these books available to anyone and everyone? It's amazing, what he's doing. And I'm thankful to be part of it."

Marco turned and looked at her as if seeing her for the first time. "What's gotten into you?" He inspected her more closely. "Did you do something different with your hair?"

She hadn't. There really was no simple explanation. She felt different. Something in her had been cracked open. She felt excited and passionate for the future—something she hadn't ever felt before. They were doing great things. The library. Sebastian. Marco. Even her own work. She wasn't sure if simply cataloguing and scribing texts alone would have brought about this change in her, but being entrusted with the Libre Vitae and carefully using what she had thought were wasted years in Latin during her school years to translate the ancient text which had lived unknown in obscurity for millennia, well, it was quite thrilling really.

She swatted Marco away. "No. I have not done anything different with my hair. Where do you want to start? With the shipment from Egypt or one of the donor shipments?"

Marco sighed and turned back toward the tower of crates. "I really should not have let it get this far behind."

"Well recrimination won't get you any further along to getting it done. How about I start with the newest shipment and you start with the oldest shipment, and we'll meet somewhere in the middle?"

Marco nodded. "You know the usual. Be sure to record the provenance and whether it needs to be scribed or moved into the IC."

He took a pry bar and began cracking open one of the shipping crates. The work was tedious but enjoyable. Marco dismantled the crates and Maeve recorded the details of each book inside the shipment. There were ten crates from Egypt alone full of weathered tomes, their bindings barely holding the fragile pages together.

During the Third World War many books had been banned and even burned in giant bonfires on the streets of various capital cities. Some fanatics erroneously thought that the old ways of things should die, but Maeve had learned that studying the old way of things was the only way to create a *new* way of doing things. If you didn't preserve the past to learn from it, you were certainly doomed to repeat it.

Others who understood the value of history and diverse points of view had started to collect books in a sort of underground book running operation. Books were funneled illegally using various underground tunnels that ran beneath cities, not just in the United State, but all over the world. Bookers, as they'd came to be called, took shipments of books and hid them away in various bunkers for safekeeping. Now, Sebastian was travelling the world and finding those shipments and sending them back to the Library for International Studies for restoration and for people to once again access the knowledge that had been deemed forbidden by the world powers.

It was satisfying work. Marco was fastidious, but he also enjoyed passing the time in conversation. He asked Maeve questions about her upbringing and schooling, and he was happy to answer her questions as well.

Marco had a similar beginning to Maeve in that he was also the result of an embryo vault. He had been quickly adopted into a family when he was just a newborn and had grown up outside of the city in a more rural area where he had learned the value of hard, honest work. His parents owned a farm and were responsible for cultivating wheat, corn and soy from seeds that had been stored in the seed vault. They also had chickens, pigs, cows, and horses. His days had consisted of waking up before sunrise and beginning his various chores around the farm. He was one of five kids, so it helped ease the burden of the work the farm involved. While he had enjoyed working on the farm, he had also yearned deeply for something more. As an avid reader, his mother had noticed this in him and he was encouraged to pursue his interests—even if that meant going to university in the city and leaving the farm behind. For now.

"Someday I think I'd like to go back. There's nothing like getting your hands dirty in the soil and seeing the rewards of your hard work. It's just not for me, at least not right now."

"Were your parents sad when you left?"

"I think my dad was a bit sad, but he's one of those stoic types, you know? Show no emotion. My mom on the other hand was a bit of a wreck. I am the baby of the family and was also the first to leave. Truth be told that made it a bit easier; knowing that my brothers and sister were still there carrying on the family business. But my mom knew that if she stifled what she called the seeker in me, that I would likely come to resent it—and them."

He began to dismantle another crate.

"Do you miss them?"

She took the packing receipt and the stack of books he handed her, set them on a table, and began recording the pertinent information into a notebook.

When she had asked that question, Marco had taken a long pause before answering.

"Only when I think about them."

After that they had worked in companionable silence for a while. Once all the crates had been opened, the items extracted, and the initial provenance recorded, Marco had wandered away to tend to matters on the above ground levels of the library.

Maeve sat down at the table to begin determining if each book was ready to be shelved, needed scribing, or additional tending to in the Immaculate Chamber.

She enjoyed the solitude, as she usually did. The basement was pleasant enough even though there was no natural light. Gaslit wall sconces were mounted along the wall and gave enough adequate light. A fireplace burned brightly and she felt right at home sitting down amongst stacks of books. A few of the crates had also contained artifacts.

Sebastian was an avid collector of various antiquities aside from books, and he was prone to sending his finds back with the books, each item carefully wrapped and placed into smaller wooden boxes within the larger crates.

She picked up one of those smaller wooden boxes now.

It smelled faintly of cedar and its sides were engraved with various hieroglyphs, except that it was a language of which she was unfamiliar. In addition to Egyptian hieroglyphics, there appeared to also be what looked like Hebrew inscriptions with its thickly lined characters and a third language similar to Hebrew but with more dots and long tails on some of the characters. She made the assumption that this was Arabic writing.

Carefully, she replicated all of the markings notating where they appeared on the box in her cataloguing notebook. The box alone was magnificent enough by itself as an artifact.

The latch was made of copper with the slightest of patina from handling.

It opened easily enough revealing a crimson satin lining. The lining had extra length so that an item placed inside could be covered from the top as well, folding the satin over the object like an infant in swaddling.

She gently moved aside the satin and her breath hitched as the box's contents were revealed. Nestled inside was a shiny gold watch. At least, it looked like a watch. Its face didn't have any numbers or hands for that matter, but it was opalescent like a black pearl and there were various inset gems: rubies, emeralds, sapphires. She had never seen something so opulent. She couldn't decide if it was old or new.

Digging in her satchel she pulled out a small magnifying glass. Picking up the watch she examined it closely. The first thing she noticed was its substantial weight. Although she hadn't doubted that the gold was authentic. It was tarnished slightly but that didn't detract from the object's beauty. She turned it over and noticed an inscription on the back, but she didn't recognize the tiny engraved characters. The symbols were more wedge-shaped than either Hebrew or Arabic, and not pictorial like the hieroglyphics. Some of the characters were also very faint as if worn away from being against the skin.

Maeve replicated what she could of the characters in her notebook and carefully sketched the watch making notations in her diagram of it.

As she set it back into the satin lining, her fingers brushed against something rough. There was something caught in the fine edge of the box where the side was dovetailed with the bottom. It was stuck between the wood interior of the box and the interior satin lining. She gave it a little tug careful not to tear it. After several seconds of manipulation, she was able to remove it only losing a tiny piece of the corner. It was a thick piece of papyrus and it too had writing, except this was a language with which she was familiar.

Ce que nous faisons maintenant résonne dans l'éternité. Avec amour.

She recognized the quote right away. It was Marcus Aurelius.

What we do now echoes in eternity. With love.

There was no name attached to the sign-off and Maeve was left to wonder if the message had been left inside the box during antiquity or if Sebastian had received such a beautiful gift from someone who not only shared his intellectual interests, but who was perhaps in love with him as well.

She quelled the strange feeling in her stomach, recorded the words from the papyrus beneath her sketch and stuck the paper back inside the box and latched it. It wasn't just jealousy that she was feeling, there was something oddly familiar about the handwriting on that papyrus. For a second, she could have sworn it was her own.

2079
GIZA, EGYPT

With Sebastian's assistance, Maeve stepped out of the small boat and onto the west bank. It was full-on evening now and the stars were out as well as a bright, full moon.

If she hadn't known better, she would have said the boat ride across the Nile was almost romantic. With the full moon glistening off the dark water and the gentle splash of the wake as they made their way across. Sebastian's arm gripping her waist—it was hard not to lose herself when she was with him. She knew their history, but he did not. His grip was more reassurance than romantic gesture, to prevent her from falling over the boat's short edge for an unexpected swim in the Nile.

Seb dropped baksheesh into the waiting hand of the boatman and thanked him in fluent Arabic before nudging

Maeve up the wooden steps built into the small hill that led from the shore toward a cluster of some buildings.

They had banked almost directly across the river at Giza. The Great Pyramid and the smaller pyramids flanking it were cast in an ethereal white glow of moonlight. Maeve could almost imagine how the white limestone had looked cloaked in the ethereal light of the moon millennia ago.

The steps gave way to a sand covered road. Even at this time in the evening people milled about experiencing moonlit tours of one of the world's most ancient sites. It was also one of the best times to do so as the dessert nights were significantly cooler than during the day.

Sebastian hadn't let go of her hand since helping her out of the boat. She noticed that the vendors usually soliciting people did not approach him, but stood back and smiled benignly. They obviously recognized and knew him so did not bother to approach. His steps were confident and sure as they walked.

The area was alive with noise: tour guides calling out, the murmurs of visitors, the sounds of those enjoying open-air dining and a late dinner or nightcap.

They wound through the city distancing themselves from the tourist-filled areas and making their way on-foot toward an area that appeared more inhabited and less visited. There were a few small shops interspersed with the dwellings. Men sat or squatted outside open doors smoking pipes and talking in rapid Arabic. Some played cards or cast dice.

Chickens pecked at the ground and the occasional mule let out a bray as they passed. Sebastian turned off the main road onto a narrower alley. The buildings were taller here and blocked out the light from the full moon. She laced her fingers through Sebastian's.

A woman leaned in a doorway, clad in a thin chemise and smoking a cigarette. Maeve could hear laughter from behind her as it flowed out the door and into the alley. The woman's kohl-lined eyes followed Sebastian as they passed, but he didn't even acknowledge her so intent on his purpose was he. When her eyes landed on Maeve, she flicked her cigarette into the alley and closed the door.

Sebastian took another turn. The narrow alleys and roadways were like a labyrinth through the ancient city. A mixture of cobblestones, dirt, and sand. The buildings here had awnings that jutted out across from either side of the alley forming a sort of canopy overhead. It was dark, but she knew that Sebastian had eyes like a cat and she had meant it when she had said that she trusted him. She knew that he would never knowingly let harm come to her.

He had been keeping a quick pace and now he slowed his steps. There was an arched alcove to the left and he gently pulled Maeve into it. A small lantern in the wall lit up an arched wooden door. She wondered if he was going to do some kind of secret knock, but instead he grinned at her, gripped the iron handle, and pushed the door open.

Golden light flooded out and nearly blinded her after being in the near darkness, but her eyes quickly adjusted as she stepped inside.

A giant lantern hung from a chain above her head and illuminated the entire space quite well. The room was full of books. Shelves lined the walls from floor to ceiling and books had overspilled from the shelves and onto the floor where there were more books in stacks of varying height from knee to hip high. The stacks of books formed pathways and she could see that there were hallways leading back to what she could only assume were even more rooms full of the same. All she could see were the books—no furniture or any other indications of life.

Sebastian grinned at her astonished reaction. "Spectacular, isn't it?"

"Spectacular is an understatement!"

Still holding her hand, he pulled her down the hallway to the left. The hallway was also lined floor to ceiling with books and created a path barely wide enough to walk through. Her brain could barely compute how this was possible. How did all these books survive? As if reading her mind, Sebastian answered her unspoken question.

"Antiquities dealers are often great appreciators of culture and the arts. While some are nefarious and deal in forgeries, others are keen on the preservation of history. Ami here is the latter."

At the end of the hallway was a doorway with a threadbare curtain pulled across it. Sebastian didn't announce their presence, but simply pushed the curtain aside and stepped in pulling Maeve in behind him.

Around Sebastian's shoulder she could see a large desk with a small lantern burning at the corner. There was a small fireplace burning brightly on the wall in front of them and to the right of the wooden desk that rather took up the majority of the small room. There was a worn armchair to the left of the desk, but like the floor and every other inch of space, it was buried under a stack of books. There was a tear along the seam of the seat cushion and batting spilled out onto the floor from the weight of the pile.

Behind the desk sat an older man hunched over a ledger. At the intrusion he looked up. His snow-white hair was shoulder length and his bifocals reflected the flame of the lantern in twin mirrors. His weathered face broke into a smile.

"Seb! Marhaba!" he bellowed in greeting rising from his seat. As he unfolded, there was the gentle creak of bone as if he had been sitting in that spot for some time. At his full height Maeve noticed he was quite tall, nearly as tall as Sebastian whose sable head nearly grazed the ceiling of the small room.

"*A-salamu alaykum*," Sebastian replied in Arabic.

"*Wa alaikum salaam*." The man replied easing around stacks of books to come out from behind his desk. Maeve noticed his long white robe flowed nearly to the floor and that he wore simple leather sandals. He also had a long graying beard nearly to the middle of his chest, which he immediately began to stroke methodically with his ink-stained hands after quickly embracing Seb. "Marhaba, Sitt." The man bowed his chin slightly in her direction.

"Ami, you old rascal. This is my friend Maeve…you know, I don't think I know your last name," Sebastian said thoughtfully. Ami's eyes flicked to their held hands and then back up to his friend's face. A small smile appeared in the beard. Sebastian had switched to English.

"A friend whose name you know not. Ah, you are always acquiring such friends. Taking them under your proverbial wing before you set them free once again," the man replied in fluent English.

"Don't listen to him, Maeve. He's always full of stuff and nonsense," Sebastian replied, but he was still smiling.

"Nice to meet you, Ami. My name is Maeve Forth."

"Ah, another American! You do have a way of collecting them, my old friend."

"Like attracts like, Ami. When we are in foreign lands it's as if the American song in our bones calls to oner another."

"May I interest you in a cup of tea, Miss Forth?" Ami asked.

"That would be lovely," she replied.

Ami began to clear the books off the armchair, but Sebastian was quicker. "Allow me, Friend." He picked up the entire stack of books that reached to just beneath his chin and moved them to another area of the room so that Maeve could have the seat.

There was a small table near the fireplace with a stack of cups and a teapot. Maeve had not previously noticed the small iron arm that could be swung into the open grate of the fire to warm a teapot or kettle. Ami poured her a small cup as well as ones for Sebastian and himself. No cream or sugar, but as she sipped the congenial beverage it was sweet with a hint of cinnamon.

Sebastian rested on the arm of the chair and Ami scooted back to his desk with his small cup.

"It was good of you to come," Ami said resuming his seat.

"You knew that I would. Your message sounded urgent in nature."

"Indeed," he absent-mindedly shuffled some papers around on his desk. "A new piece came to me quite unexpectedly. It took some time to establish the provenance, but once I had done that…I knew there was no one else to whom I could turn except to you."

"Needless to say, you have me intrigued, Ami."

Maeve noticed that Sebastian held the cup but did not sip the tea. He was close enough that she could feel the energetic excitement radiating off of him. His muscles were tensed as if ready to spring into action and she wondered what sort of antiquity could excite him so much. She thought she had an idea, but no, there was no way. It couldn't be this easy, could it?

"It is so special, so unique that I keep it under lock and key." Ami reached beneath the collar of his robe and pulled out a small key that hung on a chain around his neck. He leaned over and unlocked one of the desk drawers, rustling and moving stuff around inside before rising with a cloth-covered object in his hand.

As he handed it across the desk into Sebastian's outstretched hand, Maeve noticed that Ami's arm tremored slightly and she wondered if it was from old age or from his own excitement over this find.

"Before I take a look," Sebastian said accepting the cloth-covered bundle. "What did you establish as the provenance?"

"It goes as far back as ancient Turkey, Anatolia to be precise."

"But that's nearly five thousand years ago!" Maeve interjected.

Ami fumbled in a drawer and pulled out a pipe. He pulled out a patch of tobacco, packed his pipe and struck a match to light it. He took a long puff before he leaned back in his chair and continued.

"Are you a historian?" he asked, not rudely.

"No, not a historian. Not by trade anyways. I just love both history and art."

Ami smiled. "It's impressive to know these things. You will be a great help as Sebastian's assistant."

"I'm not—" she started to say at the same time that Sebastian replied, "She's not my assistant."

Ami's smile widened and he nodded. "I see. It stayed in Anatolia for many years. Eventually, it migrated to Europe, southern France to be more precise. According to its records, it was sold by a farmer who had found it on his land to an avid collector of ancient objects. The French collector kept it for some time before he died and his children donated many of his possessions, including the artifact to the Coptic church. It then passed hands through the church over several hundred years and covered many countries before an unfortunate fire burned one of the churches down. It fell into the hands of an opportunistic restoration archaeologist at that time whose family held onto it for many generations through the Third World War."

"What happened to if after the war? How did it get here?" Maeve leaned forward in her seat. The bundle wasn't very large. She was surprised it had traveled so many miles and passed through so many hands over the millennia. And here it was now in Sebastian's hands.

"Hard times led to the selling of it to an antiquities dealer. We need not name names." Ami puffed contentedly on his pipe. "Open it, my friend."

Sebastian carefully untied the twine and unraveled the linen wrappings.

Maeve leaned closer flushed with excitement, completely lost in the moment and forgetting that she was on an agency assignment and that her present was another two decades in the future. This wasn't her past; it was Sebastian's. But now she was not only part of his past, present, and future, but part of what she would later realize was a life-changing moment for both of them.

Finally, the object was exposed. It was small. Only slightly larger than the length and width of Sebastian's hand. It appeared to be stone. Smooth-edged like a tablet. She had seen similar in photos in books and once on a visit to a museum. The surface of the tablet was notched with a writing style that was unfamiliar to her.

"Cuneiform," Sebastian said carefully running a finger over the object's surface.

Ami smiled around his pipe, but didn't interject.

"I think I recall that form of writing," Maeve said. "It predates Egyptian hieroglyphics, right?"

"Indeed, it is one of the oldest, if not *the* oldest, systems of writing."

His sapphirine eyes moved back and forth and his mouth formed silent words. She realized that he was reading the ancient writing. The text wasn't particularly long, but when he was done reading it, he looked up and blinked as if in a daze.

"It's impossible," he whispered.

Now Ami frowned. "Not impossible. You know I am meticulous about verifying provenance, Seb. It's what differentiates me from the amateur collectors who rush around and act careless. They do not care if what they sell is fake or real as long as they make much money."

Sebastian ran his free hand through his hair and let out a breath. "I know, I know, Ami, my old friend. Indeed, it is what makes your artifacts head and shoulders above all others."

"That is why you come to me."

Maeve noticed that Sebastian was ever so slightly bouncing his knee. This was a habit she recognized from the future Sebastian. When he was excited about something the energy was difficult for him to contain. It would result in pacing or tapping, or bouncing until he could finally let the energy out.

"How much?" Sebastian asked.

"It's priceless."

"Indeed, it is priceless, but every man has a price for such a find."

"You will negotiate in front of your lady friend?"

Sebastian carefully placed the linen back around the clay tablet. "I don't need to negotiate, Ami. Name your price and the money will be delivered to you."

Modestly, Ami scribbled a price on a small piece of paper, folded it and handed it to Sebastian. He read it, but his shoulder was blocking her view, so Maeve didn't get to see. She felt him stiffen slightly and his knee stopped bouncing, but he nodded once. He tied the twine around the object and stood.

"It is done. On my honor, the money will be delivered to you within the hour."

Ami smiled around his pipe again. "It is good of you, my friend. Truthfully, I am happy to have the object gone. The weight of such a find kept me up many nights. It is better that it be with you."

He stood and the two men shook hands. Sebastian handed the object to Maeve who shrugged and placed it deep inside her satchel. Ami bowed to Maeve and wished her much health and longevity before they made their way back through the curtain and to the front of the shop.

Not until they had made their way back through the alleys and out into the city nearer to the river did Sebastian let out an emphatic whoop. He stopped suddenly, picked Maeve up around the waist and spun her around before placing her back on the ground. Instead of letting her go, he pulled her even closer and kissed her.

When he pulled back after several moments he was smiling. The built-up energy had been released and the effect had left Maeve a little light headed.

He steadied her with an arm around her waist.

"I'm sorry. That was probably a bit unexpected."

"No, it's alright. I mean, yes, it was unexpected. But it was very…enjoyable." And it was. Too bad there was no protocol for how to engage with past lovers in their past timelines. If there was a seminar at agency, that was one she must have missed. But truth be told, agency was one of the furthest things from her mind just then.

He grinned. "Well, if it was that enjoyable." He leaned his face towards hers and kissed her again. "Come on. We need to take a boat back. The nighttime rides are quite romantic. Are you staying at Shepheard's?"

She nodded dumbly as he turned and began to walk toward the bank where men waited with their boats to take people across back to Cairo. His arm was still around her and there was an extra pep in his step.

She wanted to ask what the object had read, but something told her to wait.

They easily found an available boat to take them back across the Nile to Cairo. Sebastian wasn't wrong. With the full moon and the twinkle of stars, the Great Pyramid still standing proudly despite the millennia of turmoil in the lands around it, and the soft sound of the rippling water coalescing with the pleasant hum of the boatman's humming song indeed made for a romantic ride.

The whole thing felt surreal as she nestled into Sebastian's embrace. It was like they had stolen away for a moment in time that was just for them. She wanted to remember every detail of it and not think of the future, just this blissful present moment.

They reached the east bank too soon. Sebastian dropped coins into the boatman's hand and urged Maeve up the steps back toward the sidewalk.

Despite the late hour, Cairo was abuzz with activity. The cafes were full of customers enjoying a beverage, smoking and chatting congenially. The day had cooled off with the evening and there was a pleasant breeze as they made their way toward the hotel.

Suddenly, Maeve felt herself pushed forward, stumbling to catch her balance. She felt a tug on her satchel and instinctively pulled it in closer to her body. While the strap was made of leather, she did not doubt that someone intent on stealing it could snap it.

Sebastian had dropped her hand and was now embroiled in hand-to-hand combat with the assailant. The miscreant broke free and tried to run, but Sebastian had him by the collar. He was dressed in Arabic robes, and the majority of his face was hidden by an unkept dark beard.

A crowd had gathered at the commotion. As they jostled for a better view of the action, another man in dark robes stepped forward. The moonlight glint off the blade of his knife, and Maeve had just enough time to call out a warning.

Sebastian lowered his head and gave the first attacker the full force of his shoulder, avoiding the blade that came swiping down while also disabling the first attacker. He straightened quickly and grabbed Maeve's arm, dragging her along as they ran into a nearby alley way.

They zigged and zagged through what was to her unfamiliar streets, but that seemed to Sebastian to be as familiar as the lines on his palm. She was breathing hard to keep up with him and just when she thought her heart would burst out of her chest and keep on going, Shepheard's appeared with its familiar stone façade and wrought iron gate.

Sebastian took the steps two at a time and breathlessly entered into the lobby of the grand hotel. They must have looked a fright. Maeve hadn't realized that the sleeve of her shirtwaist had become torn at the shoulder from the rough handling of her bag. She pulled out the envelope containing her key and they made their way silently up the lift to the third floor. Her room was at the end of a hallway. The doorman outside the door gave them a peculiar look, but Sebastian dropped some coins into his palm as Maeve unlocked the door and they tumbled inside, relieved.

The lanterns were already glowing and the fireplace lit anticipating her arrival. She hadn't gotten a good look at Sebastian in the commotion. She now saw that his nose was bleeding and there was a bruise blossoming at his temple. His shirt was also torn revealing the tanned sinewy musculature of his chest.

He immediately began pacing the room tightly wound as a spring. Maeve opened the door and requested chilled whiskey and glasses be brought immediately to their room. Not bothering to remove her satchel, she went to the bath chamber and dampened a wash cloth.

She handed it to Sebastian who took it and held it to his bleeding nose, not even pausing to stop his rhythmic pacing. A knock at the door indicated the delivery of the whiskey. Maeve thanked the doorman, tipped him generously, and pulled the cart inside. She filled the two glasses with ice and poured some of the amber liquid into each glass. When she handed it to Sebastian, he took a long sip then collapsed onto the divan set in front of the windows.

Taking her own glass, she sat down at the other end of the divan. The curtains were sheer and she could see out into the bustle of the city below. She realized as she took a sip that she was shaking.

Sebastian realized it too and he moved closer to her, pulling her into the crook of his arm. For a moment they just sipped their whiskey as they sat in silence. She took in the comfort of his presence next to her. She had always felt safe with Sebastian. He had always seemed to know just what to do or what to say. It was one of the magnetic things about him; rarely, if ever, had she seen him truly rattled. This was a new side of him. She also had never seen him in a fight before and she had a new appreciation for his instincts of self-preservation. As much as she thought she knew him—both in the present and in the future—he was still always catching her off guard and surprising her with new pieces of the enigmatic puzzle that was Sebastian Bates.

Finally, she felt at ease enough to ask, "They were after the tablet, weren't they?"

Sebastian's lips curled into a smile that bared all his teeth. "Ami was only too happy to be rid of the thing."

"You could read it," she said. She pulled away slightly so that she could better see his face. "What did it say?"

He moved his arm from around her shoulders to the back of the divan. Slowly, he took a sip of whiskey. His nose had stopped bleeding and the blood-spotted washcloth rested on his knee. There was some slight swelling, but instead of detracting from his appearance, it somehow gave his countenance more character.

His blue eyes narrowed as he regarded her for a moment. "Who are you?" he asked.

She bristled. "If you're implying that I am somehow in cahoots with those men, then you are sorely mistaken. I don't even know the significance of this clay tablet. Sure, I know it's old and valuable, but other than that, I know nothing. You, on the other hand, can read cuneiform and know exactly what it says. And since I was attacked and it was nearly stolen, I think that at the very least, you owe me an explanation!"

She could feel her cheeks flush as her temper rose. The sensical part of her knew that it was natural for him to be suspicious of her—she had just shown up at the museum when he was there studying the Book of the Dead in the archives and now as soon as he acquired what was a valuable antiquity, they had been attacked. He didn't know that she knew him already. Naturally, the sequence of events would seem suspect. Still, she couldn't help feeling irritated at the implied accusation.

He leaned back and closed his eyes; his lips parted in a sigh. "You're right. I apologize. You wouldn't have helped me and risked your own life, if you weren't innocent in all of this."

His eyes opened and he set his empty glass on the table beside the divan.

"You're also correct in that I could read the tablet." He gestured to her satchel, which was still strung across her shoulder. She opened the flap and pulled out the linen-wrapped bundle and handed it to him.

Again, he untied the twine and carefully removed the linen wrapping. He cradled it gently in both hands and she scooted closer to see better.

"If Ami is correct, and the provenance he gave us is true, which I believe it to be highly likely. He is a bit of a rascal, but he's the best rare books dealer in all of Cairo. I'd go even so far as to say in the eastern hemisphere. He deals fairly, but what makes him the best is his meticulous records. Before he puts something to market, he spends months, sometimes years, establishing the provenance of a find. This allows him to ask for top dollar, and his reputation over the decades has solidified his keen eye for finding invaluable texts with proven provenance."

"But this isn't a book?" The statement came out more as a question.

Sebastian chuckled. "Indeed, it is not a book...in its current iteration. This, my dear, is the very first recorded text of the Book of Life."

She couldn't help herself. "But I thought the first version was in Latin!" She quickly corrected her statement. "I mean, I assumed the oldest version would be in Latin. It seems most significant texts are. Except of course, for the Bible."

Sebastian didn't seem to notice her error, or he didn't think it significant. "Eventually, it was translated into Latin. But cuneiform is roughly 2,500 years older than Latin. As the millennia wore on, other sacred texts were added in with this one forming the Libre Vitae."

"Does this tablet have a name?" she asked leaning closer so that her nose was nearly to the wedge-shaped text. The characters were very small and the tablet was really not all that large to contain what appeared to be a lot of writing.

"It's known as the Secret of the Priests."

She looked up at him. "And what does this secret reveal exactly?"

He looked down into her face, his eyes alight with an inner fire. "It's the secret to eternal life. In other words, it explains how to become immortal."

2091
NEW YORK CITY, UNITED STATES

It didn't make any sense. The handwriting had looked just like her own, but that was clearly impossible. She could never afford such an elaborate watch! And furthermore, she would remember both purchasing it and writing the note, wouldn't she?

Maeve sat casually slouched in one of the armchairs in front of the fireplace in Sebastian's private reading room. She had been working on her translation of the Libre Vitae, but was having trouble focusing, so she poured herself a glass of wine from Sebastian's sideboard. It was late and the library was closed; Marco was long gone. It had been several months and often she wondered if he had any idea of the other project that she was working on. They were pretty good work friends, but didn't engage much outside of library hours. In fact, she knew fairly little about him except that he grew up in the country and how he came to live in the city. She vowed to change that. She couldn't spend all her free hours hunched over books and translations!

The sound of the door opening startled her before she remembered that Sebastian was returning that evening. She glanced at the clock on the mantel. His train must have gotten in late.

He didn't seem surprised to see her sitting there. "Working late?" He went to the sideboard and poured himself a glass of wine before easing into the chair across from her.

His suit was wrinkled from a long day of travel, but besides that he looked impeccable as always.

She *was* working late, but she had also been hoping to see him. It had been nearly a month since he'd taken her to that quaint French café prior to his trip, but the memory of that evening was still very vivid in Maeve's mind. There was something enigmatic about Sebastian that sparked her curiosity, but that also thrilled a small part deep inside of her. She couldn't quite put her finger on what it was.

"Trying to," she answered truthfully. "But I was having difficulties concentrating."

He laughed. "Well, that could be because it's almost midnight." She noticed he was a bit weary from traveling, but otherwise his countenance was alert. His face was tanned from his time in Egypt and the Mediterranean and it deepened the sapphire of his eyes. He looked down into his wine glass, his eye lashes were long, dark and curled. When he looked up, he had a peculiar look on his face. What he said next both excited and surprised her.

"I haven't stopped thinking of you this entire time."

She gave him an odd look. "Well, here I am now. Right in front of you."

"I know...and I'm making pleasantries like an awkward fool." He set down his wine glass and pulled her up out of the armchair wrapping his arms firmly around her waist and burying his face in her neck. When she leaned into his embrace, she felt tension release in his shoulders. He'd nearly caused her to drop her wine glass, but she was able to place it on the table before she pulled his face from the crook of her neck and held it in between her hands. He needed a shave but that was not a hindrance.

She'd wanted to say this to him since that night at the French café. "Kiss me," she said.

And he did.

It certainly wasn't her first kiss, but none of the others had felt quite like this. Her head spun and her breath shortened. She felt like her entire body was on fire. When he finally pulled away, he laughed. A sense of ease came over him.

"I have wanted to do that since the moment I first laid eyes on you. Then again that night at dinner...then going away for a month! It's been hell." His voice was rough with emotion.

She kissed him again and he pulled her down into the armchair so that she was sitting on his lap. When she had finished kissing him, he regarded her with a bemused expression.

"Beautiful, bold, intelligent...I'm not sure what I did to deserve you," he said. She blushed at the compliment feeling a trill of excitement run down her spine. Carefully (and somewhat regretfully), she extracted herself from his arms and began pacing the room behind the ornate desk where the Libre Vitae and her notes laid open.

She smiled at him. "Accept the things to which fate binds you and love the people with whom fate brings you together."

He shook his head, but finished the quote. "But do so with all your heart." He took a sip of wine and leaned back in his chair, crossing his long legs at the ankle. "Well, this last month has certainly proven that you have that."

His actions had reinvigorated her. It's as though she had been standing on a precipice. Now she knew with certainty that her feelings were reciprocated and not something she had concocted wishfully inside of her own head as she had replayed that evening in the café and subtle other things—soft words, keen looks, the gentle press of a hand on her back— leading up to it. How awful it had been to have such a splendid evening only for him to leave for a month immediately after. Now with that distraction out of the way, she felt that she could return to business.

She gestured at the open book. "Sometimes the Latin doesn't seem to translate in a way that makes sense. There are some nuances that imply this text is written by multiple authors."

He took a sip of wine and nodded. "It is a compilation of various texts over the millennia. My Latin is fair, but I mostly excel at spoken languages as opposed to the dead ones. One of my concerns, however, is that some of the things in the Libre Vitae have been, how shall we say, lost in translation."

"I agree. Having the original texts would be a great help. Most modern languages derive from Latin."

"Ah, but this text is much older than that. The origins of the Libre Vitae go back to nearly 3,000 BC."

She stopped pacing. "This text is over 5,000 years old?"

"The text, yes, the book no. Just to be clear." He finished his glass of wine and stood up. "Come with me."

"Where are we going?" She carefully closed the text, marking her page with a satin ribbon. Sebastian took the book and placed it in the safe, while she gathered her various notebooks into her satchel. Her boots were under the desk and she slipped them on and tied the laces.

"To the basement. Were you and Marco able to go through all the deliveries?"

"All, but the most recent. A couple arrived just this morning."

"Excellent, I think there is something that may help you in one of them."

They took the dumbwaiter. It rattled ominously until they reached the basement and Sebastian pushed the grate aside.

Seeing the stack of crates reminded her once again of the odd watch. She wanted to ask him about it, but a small voice inside her head told her that it would be best to wait. That small, quiet voice didn't always show up, but Maeve had learned that things worked out for the best when she heeded whatever it said. So, she would just have to quell her curiosity for the time being.

"Ah, here it is." Sebastian removed the top crate and reached for the second one. A pry bar was on the long wooden table and he used it to remove the top of the small crate. He reached inside and pulled out a long narrow wooden box and handed it to her.

It had two latches on the front and she undid them and lifted the lid. Inside was a rolled piece of parchment tied with a purple velvet ribbon.

"A scroll?" she asked.

"A key," he replied. "This scroll contains a key that should unlock the secrets of the Libre Vitae. That night," he blushed slightly. "You had mentioned the difficulties the text was presenting. I thought about it and my knowledge of the text indicates that it is best viewed as a multi-layered text. You are correct. Over the millennia the text has not only had various authors, but it also is compiled of multiple texts collected from various regions and periods of time. The Latin is an attempt to create a cohesive text."

"That makes sense and explains why it isn't a word-for-word translation. But why does it need a key?"

"Because the true secret isn't in the translation itself, but inside the code that was placed inside the text to protect its secret from people who are…let's just call them unworthy of receiving it." He smiled impishly at her.

"The Libre Vitae isn't just a sacred text, but a sacred encoded text?" She looked down at the scroll in wonder, her fingers itched to unravel it, but Sebastian reached out and carefully closed the box. He plucked it from her hands and relatched it, tucking it under his arm. Then took her by the arm and led her back to the dumbwaiter.

"Where are we going now?" she asked. Sebastian seemed to be full of surprises that evening. Any trace of weariness from his travel seemed to have disappeared.

"Home," he replied as they stepped back inside the waiting dumbwaiter. He pulled the grate closed and it rumbled back up to the main floor.

She knew she didn't need to ask, but she couldn't help teasing him just a little. "My townhome?" she asked, looking up at him coyly. His arm was around her waist and he pulled her in closer.

His eyes sparkled mischievously as he smiled down at her. "No, not this time."

***

The key was more complex than Maeve had realized. She'd been at it for a week and still hadn't broken it. This surprised her because typically she loved puzzles, especially word puzzles.

The real buster had been when Sebastian had finally let her look at the mysterious scroll. The key was only partially complete. Sebastian hadn't bothered to explain who had gotten it this far, she was inclined to believe that it wasn't a single person, but many people over a long period of time trying to crack the code. The fragile papyrus itself indicated as much.

Sunlight shone in through the window of the third floor of her townhome. It was the space she had allotted for an office. The townhome was laid out oddly. The entry level floor contained a small laundry, powder room, eat-in kitchen and living space, while the second floor had a full bathroom and two adjoining bedrooms, one of which still sat empty. The third floor was a partially finished attic space. She loved the light from the row of windows which faced the front of the house and the street below. It got the best light so she often worked and read up there. In addition to her small desk and chair, she'd moved up a battered armchair which sat beside the window, a stack of books beside it doubling as a table.

She sat in the armchair now, her legs kicked up over the arm, chewing on the end of a pencil. Before she had left

Sebastian's apartment—was that an accurate word when it was an entire floor of a building? — she had meticulously copied the key into her notebook. No way was she taking something so valuable into her possession. It was better off with Sebastian.

She was puzzling over it, when there was a knock on her door. For a moment, she thought maybe it was Sebastian, but she doubted that. She set her notebook down on the stack of books, using the pencil to mark her place and rushed down the three flights of stairs halting her momentum before she nose planted into the front door.

There was a peephole and she stood on tiptoe to see who was out there. Safety first.

Her surprise led her to unlock and yank the door open.

"Marco? Did I forget that it's Monday?"

She was dressed casually in jeans and an over-sized button-down shirt.

He looked sheepish standing on her doorstep. "No, no. It's not Monday yet. I just happened to be in the neighborhood and I knew you lived here from your paperwork...I sound like a stalker, don't I?"

Maeve laughed and rolled her eyes. "If I didn't already know that you had a photographic memory, then maybe you'd sound like a stalker. As it is, I take it that you were in this part of town, and remembering where I lived, decided to see if I was home. Well, here I am. I'm home." She gestured for him to cross the threshold but he shook his head.

"I was just wondering if maybe you wanted to take a walk and get a coffee or something? I know a nice park not far from here."

She squinted at the outside world. She had been enjoying the sunshine as she puzzled over the key. But perhaps some fresh air would do her good. It was a warm spring day and she could hear birds chirping brightly. Truthfully, she could use a break.

"Sure, let me grab a couple of things, be right back."

After she had grabbed her satchel and slipped on her boots, she found Marco sitting on her front stoop. She felt a rush of affection for him. Finally, a friend! Besides Sebastian. Although, she didn't really consider Sebastian a friend…a rush of heat flushed her cheeks.

Marco stood up and they headed down the sidewalk in the opposite direction Maeve would have taken to go to work. "There's a park down here?" she asked.

Marco laughed and shook his head. "You do live here, don't you?"

"I can't say I wander very much. Not growing up in the city, it's a little bit intimidating. I have no idea how you adapted so easily coming from the country."

"One of the first things I did was set out to find the green spaces. It's not the farm, but it helps on those rare occasions I might feel homesick."

They walked in companionable silence until they reached a little coffee stand. Marco ordered his coffee black and Maeve ordered hers with lots of cream. It really was a rather beautiful spring day. It was unseasonably warm and the sky was blue. The trees and flowers were beginning to bloom and the sun shone brightly. They took their coffee and continued to walk. Everyone seemed to be out enjoying the weather. The park was only a couple of more blocks away.

The skyline wasn't nearly the same as it had been before the war, but there were a few newer skyscrapers made of hearty stones and masonry. They passed under some scaffolding that was haphazardly constructed over the sidewalk as they crossed the street toward the entrance to the park.

The iron scroll that arched over the entrance indicated that the name of the park was Green Ways which Maeve thought was a pretty unoriginal name. It wasn't much better than naming the park after someone who had donated a bunch of money for the creation of the arch.

Marco led them to a bench that faced a large pond with mallard ducks waddling around its edge. A father with his children was apparently teaching his kids how to catch fish. The sign indicated that one should not feed the ducks, fish or other wildlife and that all fish needed to be thrown back into the water to continue the perpetuation of the ecosystem. Tall, reedy grasses surrounded the edge of the pond and in the distance, Maeve could see a little wooden shack and several small rowboats docked along the bank of the pond. Two women wearing large, floppy sunhats rode past on a tandem bike. The park was quaint and idyllic.

"This is a lovely place! I can't believe I didn't know it was here. Hard to believe I've lived here six months now." She took a sip of her coffee.

"That, my dear, is because you always have your nose either stuck in your notebook or in a book. You work longer hours than anybody I know." Marco sat beside her at a friendly distance and took a long sip of his own coffee.

"What can I say? Introvert, guilty as charged." She laughed and he smiled. The sun glinted off his wrist where he wore the odd timepiece with the large face that appeared black. Maeve had never seen it with numbers. She wondered if it could only be read in certain light. It was a peculiar watch.

"So," she asked watching as the father placed a lure onto the end of a fishing line for the smallest of his children. The metallic paint sparkled in the sunlight. "What do you do on the weekend besides come to the park?"

Marco's eyes landed on the children as well. "Mostly, I walk around the city. Sometimes I go to the museum, have you been?"

She shook her head. Surprisingly, she hadn't. She'd just been too busy. "I haven't but I know Sebastian is a patron and has a substantial collection on loan there." She said it without thinking. Marco turned toward her.

"Does he? I didn't know that. Which one is it?"

"Some of the Egyptian antiquities as well as a few Hellenistic pieces and I believe there is a clay tablet or two from the Ottoman empire…"

Marco laughed and shook his head. "Naturally. I didn't realize you enjoyed history and art so much."

She shrugged. "It's always been a natural talent of mine. I have a good memory for dates and languages. But not quite your photographic memory."

"That must be why Sebastian has stolen you away for some special project."

She had tried to limit her project to after work hours, but of course Marco would have noticed. Or Sebastian would have told him. She technically still reported to Marco and Marco to Sebastian and she did her best to protect that boundary during the work day.

"There's a text or two he's found particularly challenging," she prevaricated. "Sometimes fresh eyes are needed to see what the conditioned mind can no longer see."

Marco turned his attention back to the small family.

"And you get on well with Sebastian?"

She felt herself stiffen at the question. She could prevaricate again and reply flippantly that they got on as well as any other boss and subordinate, but something in Marco's tone of voice made her suspicious. "I'm not sure it's your business. Unless your visit today was to offer me advice?"

He whipped his head around and looked at her surprised. "Of course, you're right. It's not my business. And no, you're a grown woman and he's a grown man. I was just surprised because you seem so down to earth…"

She relaxed a little. Marco was a nice guy—a friend—and he was just looking out for her. Poor little girl with no family trying to make a living in the big bad city.

"I admire his capacity for ratiocination. His mind is quite brilliant. And, you're right, he is charming. But once you get past what seems like airs, you realize he's actually quite sincere."

"You're right," he repeated. "I don't have the right to offer you advice. But do be careful. You come from two different worlds and I would hate to see a girl like you get hurt."

"That sounds more like a cautionary tale, than advice," she pointed out.

He laughed and put a hand up in supplication. "Okay, I'll mind my own business."

"I appreciate that you consider me a friend though and want to look out for me. It's sweet," she smiled to let him know that she meant it.

"Sweet and not at all stalkerish?"

She rolled her eyes. "I never called you a stalker; you called yourself that."

He glanced at his watch, but Maeve still didn't notice any numbers or anything else on it. Maybe it was some kind of sun dial. His brow furrowed. "It's time I got going. You're good to find your own way home?"

"Through the gate, two blocks to the south and straight on until morning," she replied.

He stood up with his coffee and cast one final glance at the father and his children all happily standing knee deep in the pond with their lines cast.

"I'll see you on Monday, Maeve."

"Sounds good. Thanks for getting me out of the house, Marco. I sorely needed it." She stretched her legs out and let her head fall back so that the sun warmed her cheeks. It would make her freckly, but she didn't care.

Before Marco walked away, she thought she heard him mumble softly. "Just be careful." But she chose to pretend that she hadn't heard it, listening instead to the calm lapping of the water along the shoreline and the happy giggles of the children.

2079
CAIRO, EGYPT

The dining room at Shepheard's was full of people. Glasses clinked, forks scraped plates, and wine flowed.

Maeve was ravenous. They had slept through breakfast and lunch, and the last meal she had consumed was the previous night's mediterranean dinner. Her room only had one bedroom and Sebastian was gentleman enough to sleep on the divan with his long legs hanging off the end. She had slept deeply and soundly, reassured that Sebastian was protecting her. When she had woken up late in the afternoon, she thought he had left until she had heard the water running in the bathroom. He had stayed the entire night.

She cut into a piece of beef wellington. Shepheard's catered to tourists. If one wanted a more authentic Egyptian experience, it was best to dine off the beaten path as they had the previous evening.

"You know immortality isn't real right?"

Sebastian's eyes sparkled over his wine glass. He needed a shave and his unruly ebony hair flopped across his forehead. She always knew Sebastian to be meticulously groomed and she found this more rugged version equally as handsome, if not more so. The younger Sebastian seemed more authentic with less of a curated mask in place. She wondered what had happened between now and the present to make Sebastian feel that he required such a carefully placed mask.

"Do I?" He took a sip of wine, placed his glass on the table and took a delicate bite of his beef wellington. "The Bible indicates otherwise."

"The Bible is indicating life is eternal after the second coming of Christ and the Revelation has occurred, but we don't need to get into theological debate. Who were these priests, then?" She took a heaping bite of mashed potatoes. She didn't know how Sebastian wasn't ravenous. Maybe good breeding prevented him from devouring his plate of food like she was. Frankly, the food was delicious. Quite possibly the best she had ever tasted.

"Not 'these priests,' Maeve. But the Secret of the Priests. Think of it as an order," he corrected.

She swallowed. "Like the Knights Templar or the Freemasons?"

"Exactly," he stabbed at a green bean. "The Secret of the Priests is a little-known order more than three thousand years old. They were similar to what we would consider monks today."

"Did they have other relics?" she asked, her mind immediately jumping to such items as the Ark of the Covenant or the Spear of Destiny.

He shook his head sliding his partially empty plate carefully to the edge of the table. "No relics, only ancient scrolls and texts."

The waiter came by with a tray of cakes for dessert and Maeve helped herself to two since she couldn't decide between the triple chocolate layer cake with buttercream frosting or the strawberry shortcake trifle.

Sebastian's eyes widened. "I've never seen a woman eat so much food in a single sitting. It's quite miraculous."

She was not insulted. "I'm hungry. Not eating in so long then all that adrenaline from being almost murdered really stimulates the appetite."

Sebastian laughed and she allowed him to take a forkful of her chocolate cake.

"Now, stop trying to distract me. What do you plan to do with that text? Translate it obviously, but then what?"

He went back to sipping his wine. "Well, the clay tablet is only one of the original elements that make up the greater Libre Vitae. Once all the components were gathered, they were compiled into a common language and placed into a single, cohesive volume of work."

She finished the chocolate cake and moved on to the strawberry trifle. She already knew Sebastian wouldn't bother with that. He adored wine, chocolate and rich food. Dessert with fruit in it was beneath him.

He watched her with a bemused smile.

"By all means," she said around a mouthful of cake and cream. "Continue with your lecture."

"At some point the realization was made that should the information fall into the wrong hands the result could be…shall we say catastrophic? So, someone unknown to history decided that it would be wise to encode the secrets within the text. Naturally, they made a key. That, my dear, is the next item on my list."

Maeve swallowed the last piece of cake. She already knew that he wouldn't find the key for another decade because she had been the one to use it to decipher the Libre Vitae while working at the Bates Library for International Studies.

"So, what about the compiled text? Are you after the original components to help you better understand the Latin version?"

Sebastian stood up, placed a wad of bills onto the table, and gestured toward the French doors that led out to the terrace. She followed him. There was a refreshing cool breeze after the stifling warmth of the dining hall. The city had come alive with tourists dining or sailing on the Nile for a sunset tour. He leaned against the railing and lit a cigarette. Maeve's satchel with the tablet still tucked safely inside was slung across her body. She leaned on the railing glancing down at the people and animals below. She wasn't sure she'd ever get fully used to the unique smell and for a moment—only a moment—she wished she hadn't had two desserts.

"One reason to collect the originals is to help with the translation's accuracy. Also, I'm a collector of antiquities— legitimate ones only, of course. So, it's nice to have the originals to add to my collection." He took a long drag and let out a stream of smoke.

Her mission nudged at the back of her mind. "What about the compiled version? Don't you need that before you can bother translating it?"

He grinned in the moonlight. "Are you offering to help me?"

"It doesn't make sense to go off searching for the key to the code, if you don't yet have the book with the code in it. Do you have any leads on its whereabouts?"

He regarded her, his blue eyes bright with excitement. "A couple," he replied cooly.

"Well, then what are we waiting for?" she asked, pushing back from the railing. She pushed a little too enthusiastically and almost lost her balance, bumping into one of the nearby chairs. Sebastian caught her with one hand and she felt her breath catch as he gazed down at her. He leaned over and kissed her squarely. When he pulled back, he made a peculiar face as he helped her back onto her feet.

He took another drag of his cigarette and quirked an eyebrow at her. "I never did care much for strawberry trifle."

***

She had to remember the mission at hand. The assignment was to find out where and how Sebastian obtained the Libre Vitae. Her intellectual curiosity about the individual components from thousands of years ago warred with her determination to complete her mission.

However, her determination to complete her mission was also warring with her heart because being with this younger version of Sebastian was making her fall in love with him all over again. She was being shown a side of him she had never seen, but only heard about. She had known he travelled the world for his business, but she'd never known he was an adventurer, not simply a collector. Sometimes it felt like all the different versions of Sebastian she had known and seen ran amok in her mind clashing into one another. If she admitted it to herself, it was getting more difficult to reconcile them all.

There was something not right about the Sebastian she had seen in the future. Something that did not jive with the man she knew from the present and the past.

She tucked the thought away deep inside the recesses of her mind.

The next day after a hearty breakfast of scrambled eggs, bacon, toast and coffee—again at which Sebastian seemed amazed at the sheer quantity of which she could consume in one sitting—they headed to the train station. They were headed to Luxor which was south, and while a boat ride down the Nile would be quite romantic, they didn't have a week or more to spare. Comparatively, a train ride would be half a day.

Sebastian had insisted that they use the hotel safe at Shepheard's to stash the clay tablet. He thought it much too risky to carry it around Egypt and Maeve had reluctantly agreed with him. Being dead would certainly not help her to successfully complete her mission.

She had been able to finally change clothes when she realized that the agency had stocked the closet in her hotel room with a couple of pairs of trousers, several shirts, a khaki jacket and even a ball gown. She guessed one never knew exactly what one would run into. It had also felt delightful to wash the sand and grime from her long dark hair which in the humidity of Egypt created a frizzy halo around her head forcing her to submit it into a ponytail under her hat.

Standing on the train platform while Sebastian purchased their tickets she had the most surreal feeling. *What if,* she wondered, *I never went back? What if I just stayed here with him? What if we both just stayed here forever and never went home?*

Even as she thought it, she knew it was not only impossible, but would be catastrophic not just for hers and his timeline, but potentially for the world. She could prevent the future she had seen and tried to not think about—a future with a Sebastian she barely recognized and that frightened her. A future she didn't want not only for herself, but for Sebastian. She didn't want him to become the man she had seen.

She vaguely recalled a kind teacher at the boarding school who, when asked why there was evil in the world, replied that evil was just another tool for God to use in achieving His aim. For some reason that response had stuck with Maeve even after all these years. Could the things she had seen be used for a greater good?

She looked up as Sebastian approached. He was now cleanshaven and smoking a cigarette as he walked. People noticed him as he walked by. There was something magnetic about Sebastian Bates. She longed to pause time and just stay here with him indefinitely.

That would be breaking not just one of the rules, but *all* of the rules. And yet the thought had started the seed of an idea fermenting deep inside her heart.

"What are you thinking about?" Sebastian asked when he reached her. He was clearly oblivious to the admiring stares that followed him as he strode across the platform to her.

"Oh, nothing in particular. Just some wishful thinking."

"Wishful about me, I hope? Because you know I'm inclined to grant any and all of your wishes, Maeve Forth." He held out his elbow and she looped her arm through his.

She would just enjoy it for as long as it could last. *More importantly,* she vowed to herself, *she would remember it.*

They boarded the train. Sebastian led her to one of the overnight carriages. There was a long bench along one side and on the opposite side there were two beds attached to the wall, bunk bed style with curtains to enclose them. He stashed their valises under the bench and sat down in the corner near the window.

She sat on the bench beside him and watched the passersby in the corridor of the train through the glass of the door to their carriage. It was nearing evening and they would dine on the train, arriving in Luxor early the following morning. When she turned to him, he was staring out the window, his brow furrowed. In the distance she could see some ancient ruins and tour guides leading donkeys and camels. The sunset guided tours would be starting soon.

He seemed deep in thought, so Maeve took the moment to study him more closely. There were not yet laugh lines around his sapphirine eyes. There were no flecks of grayish white in his hair yet and his hair was longer than he wore it in the present—her present. It was slicked back now as they'd showered and he'd slicked back his curls so they were off his forehead, but she noticed in this time period he often let them run a little wild. His body was thinner and sinewy, but there was also a maturity and ruggedness about him. His jawline was angular and sitting this close she could see that his jaw was clenched, but the rest of his body appeared relaxed. He probably wasn't even twenty years old yet. When Maeve had first met Sebastian, she was only eighteen and he was about a decade her senior. Now she was nearly a decade older than the man next to her.

He turned toward her, his lips quirked in a grin. "Are you quite finished with your *étude*? If you are I suggest we make our way to the dining car so we beat the rush of other diners. We can enjoy an *aperitif*, although I'm not sure your appetite needs anymore stimulation."

She blushed at the former and rolled her eyes at the latter. "Quite. I was just noticing that you look very young. Younger than your manner would suggest."

His brow furrowed again as it had when he was looking out the window. "Does it bother you that I'm younger? I know better than to ask a lady's age, but you wouldn't bring it up otherwise."

She shook her head. "Of course not. And I'm twenty-eight. As I already said your manner suggests you're older than you appear."

He shrugged. His collar was unbuttoned almost to his chest revealing his tanned skin. He was dark enough to pass for middle eastern, especially with his ebony curls. The crocodile amulet rested in the center of his clavicle.

"I've travelled a lot, seen many things, done even more…experiencing life can make one appear older than one actually is." For the briefest of moments, a flash of uncertainty shadowed his features.

Impulsively, she took his face in her hand and kissed him gently. "I'm sorry. It doesn't bother me one bit. I didn't mean to make you uncomfortable."

At this he laughed and put his hand over hers as it still rested on his cheek. "No projecting your discomfort onto me, Maeve, my dear. Frankly, your age is the least of my concerns. Keeping your appetite satiated has become my primary concern."

She laughed. "Oh, has it? More important than cryptic ancient texts and secret codes and keys?"

He stood, pulling her to her feet with him. "Much more."

The train had begun moving as they had talked. He took her hand and opened the door out into the corridor. The dining car was several carriages over. They passed through the lounge where Sebastian stopped and ordered himself a whiskey and soda and a glass of white wine for her before they reached the dining car. Several of the tables were already occupied. He led her to a small table in the corner.

Once they were comfortably situated, she said, "So tell me about this lead you have in Luxor."

He took out his cigarette case and used the candle on the table to light the end of a cigarette. She took a sip of wine as she waited for him to answer. The one advantage she had was that she was familiar with his habits and the subtle nuances of his behavior.

"You asked about the fully assembled Latin-language Libre Vitae. As I previously explained, the book is a compilation of ancient esoteric knowledge recorded at various times throughout history, often by monks and priests, or sometimes even elders."

"The keepers of the knowledge."

He smiled as he blew out a stream of smoke. "Exactly. To me it's important to acquire the original pieces because as you know things can get lost in translation. And the more something is translated into various languages the more that can potentially be lost. Not every word can be translated literally or word-for-word."

"Or take Greek, for example," she interrupted. "Greek has something like seven different words for describing each of the various nuances of the word love. But in English we just have the one word."

He tilted his head and his eyes glittered with amusement in the candlelight. "You really are brilliant."

She flushed and took a sip of wine. "Thank you."

"But yes, you've essentially made my point for me. That's why I place such a high value on obtaining the originals. It's been damn difficult though trying to track them down."

A waiter arrived at their table and they ordered a charcuterie platter of hummus, olives, unleavened bread drizzled with olive oil, and various meats and cheeses.

Sebastian put out his cigarette and took a long drink of his whiskey and soda before he continued. "There's an eccentric antiquities dealer in Luxor. Like our friend Ami he specializes only in ancient texts. His name is Ludwig and he's an expat from Germany. He came to Egypt when he was a young archaeologist. But there was an incident on one of his digs. An opening hadn't been shored up properly and it collapsed, killing several of his men, and badly injuring Ludwig. He had quite a severe head injury and while he's physically fully recovered, he never was quite the same mentally. He gave up archaeology and took up collecting instead."

"That's both horrible and tragically sad," Maeve said as the waiter returned and laid out various plates of food across their small table.

Sebastian nodded as he unfolded his napkin and draped it across his lap. "I agree. He's a good man, Ludwig. Talks a bit in riddles and circles sometimes. Keeps to himself."

Maeve helped herself to some pita bread dipped in hummus. "So, we are going to visit Ludwig?"

"That is one stop. The other is a curator in the Luxor Museum of Art," Sebastian popped several pieces of cheese into his mouth. "It's good to show my face there once in a while. I'm a patron of the arts and donate a lot of my money to the cause of art preservation."

She smiled. That was not all that different from the Sebastian she knew. However, she realized she actually knew very little about the truth of his background and how he came into his wealth at such a young age. She'd assumed it was because of the death of his father. It surprised her that a young bachelor would spend his fortune on antiquities and the preservation of art and history, or the acquisition of books far and wide to make them available to the public.

"I'm sure visitors to the museum that experience your patronage appreciate your dedication to the cause."

Sebastian looked thoughtful. "That is the hope. I know what you're thinking because I can see it in your eyes. Really, you should work harder on disguising your countenance. You're wondering how someone as young as myself has so much wealth."

She must have looked shocked because he laughed. It wasn't that her face was so easily read; it was that Sebastian had always been able to know her innermost thoughts. It was one of his more peculiar talents.

"After the Third World War, my father was a large investor in oil, steam and coal. He knew that it had worked several centuries before and that it would likely work again. It turned out in this case that history did indeed repeat itself. He put forth all of his capital and was rewarded tenfold. I'm an only child and my parents died in an unfortunate accident when I was about eight years old. They were on a trip and I was away at boarding school overseas. They were traveling through the Alps and there was an avalanche. It trapped the train and it was a remote area, difficult to deploy resources to provide aid. By the time helped arrived, it had been over a week with no heat, little food and little fresh water. They, along with all the other passengers, perished."

Maeve looked out the window of the dining car at the darkening desert landscape.

"I'm so sorry," she replied.

Sebastian shrugged. "My fortune was put into a trust until I came of age, which in this case was at sixteen years according to my father's request."

She had never heard this story and it tugged at something deep inside her. Even though she had fallen in love with Sebastian and believed that he had loved her in return, and despite his many travels and connections around the world, she realized that his life must be a particularly lonely one.

"That seems like a lot of responsibility for a young man," she finally said.

"It was...is, but I think I've gotten the hang of it now. My father was an astute businessman and he taught me much of what he knew. The remainder was rounded out with an education at Yale University. I realized that the money I made could make me a very comfortable life, but that it could also help other people. There was also enough that I could travel and perhaps engage in a little quest. An idle mind never leads to anything good." He smiled wolfishly and lit another cigarette.

"So, searching for the Libre Vitae—is that your quest? Like some Homerian hero?"

He let out a ring of smoke. "My quest isn't just the search for the book, of course. But for the knowledge inside of it."

"A quest for immorality then?" she took another sip of wine and a nibble of cheese.

"That sounds much more epic than my humble efforts."

She smiled. "Everyone needs a purpose."

He looked thoughtful again and took a long inhale of his cigarette then a long exhale. "Does that make you the maiden that's come to assist me on my quest?"

"Something like that."

He raised an eyebrow. "I hope you've read enough epic quests to know that often the hero has a torrid, passionate affair with said maiden."

She laughed. "And her undying love and loyalty for the hero spur him on during his quest despite any obstacles and difficulties he might face. The remembrance of her beauty like Helen of Troy launching a thousand ships, and his longing to hold her in his arms once again after all the battles were won and he returns home!" She really had read too many epics.

Sebastian put out his cigarette, downed the remainder of his whiskey and soda, then abruptly pushed back his chair and stood up. He held out a hand across the table.

"Perhaps it's a good time to return to our carriage for the remainder of the evening," he said in a soft voice.

Maeve recognized the tone. She stood up and placed her hand trustingly in his. Sebastian had always been a bit of a romantic and she expected no less from his younger self.

100 AD
GAUL, ROMAN EMPIRE

The church glowed with candlelight. All was silent except the soft dragging of the monk's robes across the stone floor. It was midnight and his brothers were asleep in the monastery at the other end of the gardens.

His arthritic knees required that he walk slowly, but he was not in a hurry as he knew exactly where he was going.

He carefully made his way down the aisle running through the middle of the church with the old wooden pews flanking either side. Above him the ceiling rose to mountainous heights and resembled the bottom of a ship with its ornate wooden beams. He proceeded slowly toward the nave which housed the altar of the church, a simple limestone structure with the great holy book resting on a gilded tray.

Behind the pulpit he entered into an alcove that was covered with a thick velvet curtain of the deepest and richest amethyst. The alcove held a shelf containing only a gold, jewel-encrusted chalice and a matching dish. But it was the floor of the alcove that held the monk's interest.

His knobby fingers felt blindly for the groove in the stone, and finding it he pulled with all his might until the wooden door embedded in the floor creaked with movement. He slid it off to the side. From the pocket of his robe, he removed a roughly formed tallow candle and stepped out of the alcove to light it with the flame from one of the nearby sconces. He gently pushed aside the thick curtain so it wouldn't catch the flame and edged his body into the opening that was now revealed in the floor.

The first few steps were the most difficult, but his slippered-foot found purchase effortlessly from decades of memory.

A shallow pool of light from the candle only illumined the next step. He was not in any particular rush, so he moved slowly and carefully down the steps until he found the change to dirt underfoot.

The stairwell opened onto a corridor, its walls and ceiling painstakingly carved out by ancient hands. Few knew of the array of tunnels that crisscrossed beneath their feet in every major city around the world. This particular tunnel dated back to antiquity, but the monk was familiar. His feet guided him without much thought from his head. He had been the keeper for many years, but once again persecution loomed. It seemed that it always did, just as the Lord had predicted for his followers. Rather than have this treasure fall into the wrong hands, the monk had decided to hide it away so that when the timing was right, it could once again be found.

The tunnel snaked left and right, created to disorient those who should not be inside it. At various points the tunnel looked as though it split off, but the explorer would either eventually run into a dead end in a side tunnel with a wall of compacted dirt, or he would experience a U-shaped side tunnel that ended up back inside the main tunnel. One could spend hours going in circles beneath the church.

There was the rustle of something scurrying, but the monk did not react. He was quite used to the sounds of the tunnels. The vermin that had made it home, the occasional bird or bat who had somehow wandered inside.

By the time he reached his destination the candle had burned low. He paused to light a new one and snuffed out the other against the stone wall leaving a smudge of soot before dropping the used candle into the pocket of his woolen robe.

Here is where the tunnel opened into a chamber. The chamber was not particularly large. There were rough-hewn dirt shelves in every wall of the chamber and they were full of bones and skulls with hollow eyes that leered eerily in the candle light.

If someone had made it this far, the mere sight would likely drop them into a faint or otherwise send them running for escape back to the above ground world.

The monk was at peace with the dead. The dead were good at keeping his secrets.

The bones were arranged thoughtfully and the skulls peered out like sentries from their shelves. On the floor was a large wooden trunk with an iron lock. The trunk was knee height and about three feet in width. An inset in the top of the trunk had hand-carved words in-laid with ivory and written in Latin: *Qui quaerit non inveniet. Qui invenit, cognoscet in aeternum.*

He who seeks shall never find. He who finds shall forever know.

He used some of the burning candle's dripping wax to create a small pool on the dirt floor with which he could place his candle momentarily and still use its light.

With shaking hands, the monk pulled a cord hidden beneath his robe that hung around his neck. It held a small iron key only the length and width of his index finger. He inserted the key into the lock and heaved open the heavy lid of the trunk. Inside it was lined with ruby red velvet, but otherwise it was empty.

From his robe, he removed a small book. Its cover was made of supple leather and was decorated in embossed symbols gilded with gold leaf. He delicately placed it within the velvet lining, tucking it in as he would a small child into a bed for the night. Before he closed the lid, he patted the book lovingly and whispered a prayer in guttural Latin. Then he brought the heavy lid back down and turned the key in the lock. But instead of placing the key back around his neck he stood up and went to one of the shelves. He moved aside one of the skulls—this one with a fracture down the right hand side as if an ax had come down on the unfortunate soul's head.

His knobby fingers worked at the dirt until he had created a shallow hole in which he placed the key, then he moved the dirt back over it giving it a final pat before he returned the skull to its original resting place. He retrieved his candle which was now half burned down. He had only brought two and he had just enough left to make it back to the entrance in the alcove before it would be gone.

He bowed slightly at the chamber entrance to the dead who would keep watch over his treasure.

As he made his way back through the tunnel he noticed an additional sound that seemed out of place. His hearing was no longer as strong as it had been in his younger years, but he noticed it was not the familiar scurrying of mice or rats, but a faint scratching. Still he kept walking. He did not alter his pace and his heartbeat was slow and steady. Deep inside he seemed to already know what awaited him when he would reach the top of the stairs. He was not afraid. He had made his peace with death long ago and knew that his soul's eternal life with the Lord was more precious than the fleeting moments spent here on earth with those who denied their own Divine nature.

The candle burned his fingertips as he finally reached the wooden stairs. He climbed up whispering the Lord's prayer to himself. When he reached the opening at the top, it was as he had expected. In his ill eyesight he only saw the shadows hovering in the darkness—not one, but two. So they think I am worthy of two, he had thought as his head emerged from the opening. Before the shadows encompassed him, he tossed his candle at the velvet curtain in the alcove. It was just enough that the burning flame caught the corner of the curtain. Fire began to eat at the fabric.

The monk smiled in satisfaction and that was the last thing he remembered before he felt a sharp pain in his head and another in his back between his shoulder blades and everything returned to everlasting darkness.

2092
NEW YORK CITY, UNITED STATES

The new year had came and gone. Glitter, sparkle, champagne and festive cheer were replaced with a thick gray cloud layer, freezing cold temperatures, and somber moods.

Maeve was sitting in her office. She used the tern loosely. In size it was not much better than Marco's closet-sized office, however, she lucked out in that her office was not located in the basement, but on the half floor with the Immaculate Chamber and near Sebastian's office. It was quieter than the basement since there weren't deliveries being made and she couldn't hear the prattle of the dumbwaiter. She also had been fortunate that it had a window—it wasn't as luxurious as Sebastian's office or reading room, which she had quite taken over with her books and papers...and shoes, but it was her own little space. Sometimes she still found herself up in the reading room late into the evenings because the fire was cozy when Sebastian wasn't there and when he was she rather enjoyed his company.

Here, her desk was a simple round oak table and the chair was an upholstered one she had pulled from one of the common areas figuring no one would really notice its absence. She sat facing the window which looked out onto the street and the cemetery across the way, but half of her view was blocked by the dark green awning of the building next door.

Currently, she was going through the library catalogue trying to notate gaps in the collection. It was done quarterly and it was necessary work, but it was one of the more boring tasks and hard as she tried, she couldn't keep her mind from wandering. Her cup of coffee had long ago gone cold.

It was bittersweet that the holidays had come and gone. This had been her best Christmas and New Years yet. She had spent Christmas Day with Marco because Sebastian was out of town. There had been a lot of snow, so Marco hadn't ventured out into the countryside to visit his family. Instead they had stayed in sipping hot cocoa and doing a five-thousand piece puzzle. They still hadn't finished it. He had gifted her a new moleskin notebook in a rich amber color and she had gotten him a cashmere scarf in a shade of drab green, but it brought out the green flecks in his brown eyes and suited his tousled brown hair. It had been a lot of fun and sometimes she thought her cheeks still hurt from laughing so much at Marco's bad jokes.

Sebastian had come back into town from Paris in the week between Christmas and New Year's Eve. He had asked her to spend New Year's Eve with him and she didn't hesitate when she said yes.

She had been nervous when Sebastian had insisted on sending a motorcar to pick her up. It was sleek black with tinted windows and she had never been in something so luxurious (or frivolous). The driver had been friendly and the ride short when they had pulled up to Sebastian's other house an hour outside of the city, which was five times the size of her own small townhouse in the city. It was different than the modern penthouse apartment he kept near the library; this house was all stone work and board and batten with a slate roof and a tall limestone wall that enclosed the grounds. Even in the fallow season she could see the evidence of extensive gardens as they drove up the lane to the house. It reminded Maeve of something out of a fairy tale.

Now she replayed the evening over in her mind. He'd given her a first edition of Marcus Aurelius's *Meditations*. That had nearly taken her breath away, but what really took it away was that Sebastian had filled the small book up with pieces of paper containing his comments and notes—things he wanted to draw her attention to. She had never received such a gift before and it overwhelmed her to realize that he knew her so well. That evening she'd also learned that Sebastian was an excellent chef. She realized that he didn't regularly cook for lack of any skill of his own, but because he didn't often have the time he thought should be invested when creating a meal. The evening had been slow and languorous; they rang in the new year with champagne and a kiss that certainly promised 2092 was going to be a very good year indeed.

Movement on the street below caught her eye and reluctantly took her out of her reverie. She thought she had seen...there it was. Just the flicker of drab green. She peered down at the street below and saw Marco with his coat buttoned up and his new scarf wound around his neck and over the bottom half of his face. They were experiencing a brutal cold snap. He was standing nearly obscured by a large delivery truck and if not for the green of his scarf, she would have completely missed seeing him. She was about to tap on the glass to draw his attention, when something strange happened.

He looked down at his watch then glanced furtively around before tapping its face. And then he disappeared. Out of thin air.

Maeve stood up so quickly she nearly knocked over the cold coffee. She settled it with an outstretched hand as she pressed her nose to the window. The delivery truck pulled away. Marco was not there.

Had she imagined him standing there? She had been daydreaming after all, perhaps it was her subconscious projecting the image of Marco onto the street below. She immediately dismissed the rationalization as blatantly ridiculous. If her subconscious was going to conjure up anyone, it would be Sebastian not Marco. No offense to Marco.

She rubbed her eyes and squinted at the overcast landscape. The small cemetery was empty, except for those enterally resting, and there was definitely no sign of Marco. They had an internal phone system in the library and Maeve picked up the receiver and dialed the number to Marco's office. She let it ring ten times before hanging up.

Annoyed, but thankful for the interruption to the monotony of what she was supposed to be doing, she decided she'd better go down and check for herself. Just because Marco didn't answer his phone didn't mean he wasn't wandering around somewhere in the basement. He just had been too far away to hear it ringing. That must be it. Maybe she had just seen a young man who resembled Marco with his too long brown hair that never stayed put, and the same worn brown wool coat...and the same drab green cashmere scarf.

She sighed and rested her forehead against the window's glass. It was freezing. No, why lie to herself? She had most definitely seen Marco. There was no use doubting what her eyes had seen. She had a keen sense for details and often noticed what others overlooked. It was the same reason Sebastian had entrusted her with Libre Vitae and the codex. She had seen what she had seen. There was no two ways about it.

But admitting that raised more questions than answers. Where had Marco gone? And more importantly, what was that device?

2079
LUXOR, EGYPT

Luxor had a more genteel air about it than Cairo. Although, Maeve will admit that her first impressions were colored by the fact that she had woken up pleasantly in the embrace of Sebastian's secure arms that morning.

The Winter Palace was only a short cab ride from the train station and Maeve's mouth gaped in amazement when they pulled up to the impressive facade. Its creamy yellow stone work and dramatic curved double staircase flanking the columned entrance stood commandingly on the eastern shore of the Nile. Sebastian had explained that the original structure was built in the late nineteenth century and had been added onto over the subsequent centuries. Before the Third World

War there had been a horrible fire and while the majority of the outside building had been undamaged, the inside had experienced significant damage.

Still, when she walked in through the ten-foot-tall double doors and into the lobby with its black and white checked marble floors and opulent chandelier with dangling crystals to say she had been impressed was an understatement.

Even as a young man, Sebastian didn't lack confidence. He marched right up to the front desk with Maeve in tow and demanded the best room available. As soon as he said his name, the clerk had begun to perspire ever so slightly and kept referring to Sebastian as Bates Effendi, a sign of both respect and Sebastian's level of education and influence.

A room had been procured almost instantly. They took the stairs to the second floor and a baggage clerk dropped their small valises inside the entry before bowing himself out after Sebastian dropped some coins into his outstretched palm.

Maeve stepped into the room. It was decorated in dark woods and brocade. All the colors were of varying rich gemstone tones. The windows looked out onto a spattering of palm trees and the Nile glistening in the sun. People were already heading out on foot or boat to visit the various temples before the afternoon sun made it nearly unbearable.

The room itself had a small living space with a divan and two elegantly upholstered chairs and a breakfast table. Off of the little living space was a bedroom with two queen-sized beds and an adjoining bath chamber with a free-standing claw foot tub and a small shower with beautiful handmade tiles in a Moroccan print. She hadn't ever stayed in a place this luxurious. Because of the sequence of events, she'd barely even had a chance to sleep in her room at Shepheard's before she was haring off on an adventure. Not that she was complaining.

"Not bad, eh?" Sebastian asked. He hadn't sat down yet but was studying her curiously.

"It's magnificent." She stepped back toward the window. "And the view is equally so."

He came and stood beside her, his shoulder pressed against hers. "I'm sorry we don't have time for me to show you around. I may be biased, but I do think I'm the best tour guide around, and I feel certain you'd love the Temple of Hatshepsut, but it's several hours away."

"The queen who wore the beard of the pharaoh and whose reign they tried to wipe from history?"

He put his arm around her shoulders and affectionately kissed the top of her head. "Have I told you that you're brilliant?"

She laughed. "Only about half a dozen times."

"Well, it's only because it's the truth."

He pulled away and began pacing. "So, first things first, the museum is only a couple of blocks from here, so I think we should drop in there. We don't need to be there long; it's more to show my face than anything. Then we can visit that old rascal, Ludwig."

It was strange to watch him. His mannerisms hadn't changed much in twenty years and when he spoke, he sounded much older than the young man that he was.

He stopped pacing and quirked his eyebrow at her. "You're doing it again. Staring at me with that peculiar expression...as if..." He laughed and shook his head then mumbled, "But that's impossible."

She stepped forward away from the window and pressed her palms against his chest. His eyes were an endless sea of blue. "What's impossible?" she asked. Her breath hitched in her chest.

"You look at me as if you know me."

Lying to him felt wrong, so she settled for a half-truth. "You're familiar to me, that's all." She moved her arms up around his neck and pulled his face towards hers and kissed him. After several minutes, he pulled back and chuckled, but he didn't let go of her waist.

"Okay, I know that you're trying to distract me and I must admit you're doing a fabulous job at it. But I refuse to let you deter me from the greater mission at large."

Maeve pulled away satisfied that she had successfully stopped his line of inquiry. However, she knew that stopping it and Sebastian forgetting it were two very different things and that the latter was highly unlikely.

"By all means. The maiden should never distract the hero from his epic quest."

***

The Luxor Museum of Art was not what Maeve had expected. She had expected antiquity, but what she got was what Sebastian referred to as a modern monstrosity. Whereas she had hoped for a building resembling one of the nearby temples, she was instead presented with lots of metal and glass that glared blindingly in the late morning sun.

Sebastian reassured her that there were actual antiquities inside and that they did in fact have their own entire wing because he had been the one to fund it.

The sharp angles and modern exterior seemed out of place in the ancient ruins of Luxor and she wondered who had commissioned the architect that had created something so horrendous against the beautiful landscape around them. Unfortunately, the inside was not much better.

Despite all that glass on the outside, inside had been tinted so that the natural light entering the building was filtered. The effect was like that of an overcast day.

A concierge ran around from the curved marble counter in the center of the museum's foyer, but Sebastian craftily side-stepped him and grasped Maeve's arm with a smile, directing her to a wide set of black marble stairs just behind the concierge's information station.

"In a bit of a hurry, mate. The lady is dying to see the antiquities wing. Can barely hold her back!"

Maeve threw the gentleman, whose mustache seemed to droop along with the rest of him at Sebastian's dismissive greeting, an apologetic smile and let herself be pulled along. He was moving so swiftly she wasn't even sure her feet were touching the ground.

At the top of the grand staircase, there was an untinted sky light that allowed natural, unfiltered light to pour into the space below, creating a single rectangle of golden sunlight on the floor right at the center. Beyond was the antiquities wing.

"I insisted on installing that skylight. This place is right gloomy considering that it contains art and artifacts that are supposed to move the soul."

He moved his hand from her elbow to the small of her back and guided her farther into the wing. The entrance into the wing was a giant cased opening and she noticed a small, sleek black plaque with silver lettering indicating that the wing had been the generous donation of Sebastian Bates.

Once beyond the opening her mouth hung agape. There were Egyptian busts in glass cases resting atop chest height pedestals, slabs of stone with petroglyphs were mounted to the walls, long cases held smaller artifacts of scrolls, amulets, rings, chest plates, and other jewelry. And it wasn't just Egyptian, she noticed there were Ottoman and Aztec artifacts, Native American, African, East Indian and Asian. It was a smorgasbord of the world in one small room, well not too small, it was actually quite large all things considered.

Once she got over her initial shock, she found words. "All of this is yours? It's unreal."

He looked rather sheepish. "Actually, it's just part of a larger collection. Some of my favorite pieces are on display at my house in the states, some of the more fragile pieces are in storage waiting restoration, and some pieces are on loan to other museums. But this is the only museum where my collection takes up an entire wing."

She moved toward a long case against the far wall. It was filled with papyri, scrolls, and small clay tablets. "Have you been collecting since you were an infant? It seems impossible one person could have acquired so much..."

He followed her and peered down into the case. "The majority of it was part of my inheritance, but I have been known to alleviate the more scrupulous dealers of their most prized artifacts to ensure that they're in safer and better hands. Available for all to enjoy and learn from as opposed to sitting in some pompous tycoon's study hidden away from the world."

"Tell me how you really feel, Sebastian." A sharp female voice infiltrated their conversation.

Maeve looked up from the clay tablet she had been inspecting through the glass to find a woman standing about five feet behind them. She had on extremely high heeled white pumps with a pointed toe and wore a bright yellow linen pant suit that complemented her deeply tanned skin and hair so pale blonde that it was almost white. Her eyes were a faded cornflower blue and her lips were painted with garish bright pink lipstick. A tropical printed scarf was knotted around her slender, tanned throat.

Sebastian took his time turning around and Maeve immediately noticed that his normally bright eyes took on a darker more malevolent hue.

"Abigail, it's so good to see you." He smiled, but Maeve didn't believe him for a second when he said the words.

"Liar," Abigail replied. She smiled as well, but it seemed a forced expression revealing perfect white teeth. She stepped forward and extended a hand toward Maeve. Maeve felt Sebastian stiffen ever so slightly next to her. "Abigail Young, curator for the Luxor Museum of Art and Artifacts."

Maeve wasn't sure what to do in this situation. There was obviously some weird dynamic happening, but she wasn't a heathen so she stuck out her hand and introduced herself.

"Maeve Forth...uh...adventurer."

She said it with more confidence than she felt. And surely introducing herself as a Secret Government Time Travelling Agent was off the table, nor could she introduce herself as Sebastian's Research Assistant because he hadn't experienced that yet in his timeline.

Abigail's handshake was firm and she squeezed a little too hard for what Maeve considered appropriate. She noticed that her nails were perfectly groomed and painted a pink that matched her lipstick.

"Adventurer? How...unique."

When Maeve got her hand back, she ignored the little half-moons that had been inflicted.

"What she means is that she's a traveler and a researcher. She's working on her post doctorate and a colleague recommended her. We met up in Cairo then travelled down to Luxor together." Sebastian lied smoothly and it surprised Maeve how the lie wasn't actually all that dissimilar from the truth. Well, except the post doctorate part. But she certainly was both a researcher and a traveler, just not the type of traveler that someone like Abigail would expect.

Abigail's smile grew wider and it appeared to now be pasted onto her face which made it lose some of its faux pleasantness. Maeve suspected they were around the same age give or take a couple of years.

"How lovely. What is your post doctorate research in?"

"Sacred texts and rituals of the priest class in the Ottoman and Roman Empires." The half-truth spilled from her lips so easily Maeve surprised herself. Possibly because it was more truth than lie.

"I see. That sounds quite interesting. I'm sure Sebastian would love the opportunity to lean into your expertise."

Suddenly, Maeve had the oddest feeling that Abigail was not talking about research. This striking blonde woman that was the curator for an entire museum appeared to be jealous of her. Was Sebastian a former lover? Or was it a love that was unrequited? Maeve wasn't the jealous type, so her curiosity was just that.

Sebastian returned his hand to the small of Maeve's back. Her own linen shirt was stuck to her skin with sweat. Everywhere in Egypt was hot and humid. Or both. Maeve hadn't stopped sweating since she'd arrived.

Abigail's pale eyes didn't miss the gesture and they narrowed ever so slightly, framed by perfectly manicured eyebrows. Something about Abigail Young gave Maeve an ominous feeling. She just didn't know if it was an ominous present feeling or future feeling.

"We really have to run. We are meeting an old friend for brunch. The collection looks outstanding, aside from that smudge on the glass of the manuscripts case. But I'm sure you'll see to that." Sebastian's remark was borderline rude.

He nudged Maeve forward and around Abigail and back out of the wing before heading to the left and entering a stairwell. The stairwell led them down but Sebastian didn't stop at the ground level. Instead, he kept proceeding downward two more levels before he finally came to a stop.

"An ex-paramour?" Maeve couldn't help asking.

"Jealous?" he grinned at her with a glint in his eye.

"Hardly," Maeve rolled her eyes and Sebastian kissed her with such intensity that if she had been jealous any remnant of it would have been forgotten.

When he was finished, he pulled back and looked at her meaningful. "Don't be."

With that he pushed open the door she had been leaning against and caught her before she could fall backward into the room behind it.

They had exited out of a stairway and into the museum's basement. It reminded Maeve of the Bates Library for International Studies basement except instead of books it was full of large pieces draped in dust protecting canvases. From their shapes she could identify which were pieces of wall art and which were sculptures.

"Back here," Sebastian directed. There were narrow windows that let in scant sunlight lining the walls, but it was enough by which to see as they navigated a narrow aisle of shelves lined with boxes and crates.

"Isn't it risky to just leave the door to all of this unlocked?" she asked. She noticed a bust that reminded her of the work of Leonardo Da Vinci. Its canvas drape had slid off and was hanging precariously on the corner of its pedestal.

"It was locked," Sebastian replied. He held up a small key and Maeve realized that when he'd kissed her and pushed her up against the door, he had also unlocked the door at the same time. She'd been too pre-occupied to even notice.

He made his way to the far corner of the room where there was a cobwebby wooden shelf. It was lined with boxes. The boxes were labeled with dates, locations, and what appeared to be last names. Donations of artifacts?

She knew Sebastian had those cat eyes and as he proceeded from one set of windows and toward the others, he squinted in the dimness as he examined the labels.

"Ah, here we go." The box he pulled out was the size of a shoe box. He tucked it under his arm and continued down the aisle. When they reached the end, he turned right and Maeve noticed they were back where they had started.

Sebastian locked the door behind them and they headed back up the stairwell, but instead of returning out the main entrance, they took a narrow hallway that ended in a door marked STAFF ENTRANCE. It deposited them at the back of the museum.

The sun was glaring after the dim basement and filtered light inside the museum.

"Are you going to tell me what's in that box you just stole?" Maeve asked as they walked farther away from the museum and back into the bustle of the city. It was mid-morning and both tourists and vendors were out in full swing.

"Not stolen. Borrowed. Besides, it's actually my box. It's pretty difficult to steal one's own property. Even you couldn't argue with me about that." He tipped the box in her direction. "See, my name's right there."

And he wasn't lying. The label clearly had Bates written across the bottom beneath the words ROMAN EMPIRE and RELIGIOUS TEXT and CIRCA 100 AD. However, even though he was the sole living Bates; he was not the only Bates to have ever lived. The box very well could have belonged to his father. Still, she supposed he was right, even if it were a family heirloom, that it wasn't technically stealing if it was one's own property.

"You didn't answer my question," she said shaking her head at a vendor offering her bouquets of brightly colored purple and yellow flowers.

"I'm famished. I wasn't completely fibbing when I mentioned we were late for brunch. I know you have to be hungry. You're always hungry. How about we get something to eat before we find Ludwig? There's a strong possibility once we find him, we won't get rid of him easily and it will most likely cut into the lunch hour."

"I am not *always* hungry," she replied. He tilted his head and looked at her sideways. "I just happen to appreciate various cuisines and the sensible delicacies that they offer."

"Come on. I know a place that won't be drowning in tourists."

"And then will you show me what's in the box?"

"Maybe. It depends on if you eat all of my zalabia or not."

***

It turned out zalabia was amazing. It was roughly equivalent to an American donut, but oh, so much better. It was a fried dough and the result were fluffy balls that were both crunchy and sweet. It was covered with powdered sugar and served with little ramekins of both melted chocolate and caramel.

As far as Maeve was concerned it was a little piece of heaven to please mere mortals.

She had to admit that Sebastian knew all of the best places for meals. There were few tourists who didn't stick to the more obvious cafes and restaurants, places that also provided a dose of Westernized options. Maeve was more than happy to adventure into more authentic fare.

Her belly was full and her mind was ready. Despite her zeal for zalabia, she had not forgotten about the box Sebastian had borrowed from the museum. Although, he was correct that if it was his property on loan to the museum, it wasn't technically stealing, she still felt a little uneasy about it.

Sebastian sipped his coffee, sitting back with his long legs crossed at the ankle. He really was in his element and she found that she loved this young adventurer side of his personality. She found herself wondering when and why he had abandoned the lifestyle.

He had pulled a slim metal case out of his pocket and was about to light a cigarette when he caught the stricken expression on Maeve's face and laughed out loud.

"Okay, okay. Don't look so terrorized. We can open the box now."

She scowled. "I was not terrorized."

He put the unlit cigarette behind his ear. "If curiosity ever killed the cat, I'd suspect that you have nine lives."

He pulled the box over from the edge of the table. They were sitting inside the restaurant next to a large window that had no glass and was completely open to allow the breeze inside. Beneath the windows were cobblestones and beyond that a line of Tea Roses that appeared to be well-tended. To steal the box—if someone knew that they had it and where it was—someone would have had to trample through the roses, reach in the window, and pluck it from the table which Maeve was certain would have landed them with a knife point through the delicate flesh and bones of the hand.

As it was, few people walked by because the cafe was tucked back amongst small houses in a residential area. Naturally, Sebastian was on a first name basis with the proprietor, the proprietor's wife and each of their ten children who all had come out with copious greetings for their favorite patron.

The box was long and narrow and non-descript. It wasn't even locked or sealed in anyway. Gently, Sebastian lifted the lid and placed it to the side. Maeve leaned forward, her hair dangling precariously over her cup of unfinished coffee.

Sebastian nudged the box closer to her side of the table and she peered inside. He smiled, sat back and resumed lighting his cigarette.

Inside the box was a piece of parchment. It was charred around two of the edges as if it had survived a fire, but one of the longer sides had a ragged edge that clearly indicated it had been torn out of something. Her expert eyes saw faint evidence of the threads of string which was commonly used in binding materials before glues and adhesives became ubiquitous.

The characters on the page were small and black. And familiar.

Maeve reached into her satchel and pulled out a small magnifying glass. She peered at the text then looked up at Sebastian with a startled expression. "It's in Latin."

He blew out a stream of smoke and nodded once, but his eyes betrayed his calm demeanor. The sapphirine blue was all but dancing.

She looked at it again, pulling the box closer and leaning over it with her magnifying glass. Recalling the label on the side of box indicating that the contents were a religious text from 100 AD in the region of Gaul, which was modern day France, but in 100 AD part of the Roman Empire, her heart began to beat faster and her palm holding the magnifying glass became clammy.

Christians in the Roman Empire used Latin. And 100 AD meant this was less than a century after Christ had walked the earth. If she had been in a room by herself examining such a text she would have been unable to squelch her squeal of delight. As it was, she breathed out slowly through her nose, afraid that the slightest bit of carbon monoxide would crumble the text before her very eyes. This parchment was almost 2,000 years old.

Luckily for her, she also could sight read Latin. Parts of the text were missing, either disappearing in the charred off bits or being torn when the page was removed from whatever larger work it had once been a part of.

Her eyes scanned and her lips moved silently as she read the small print with its careful black strokes. But there was no way. She read it again more quickly this time then looked up at Sebastian unable to hide her surprise.

"This is impossible."

He smiled. "Oh, I assure you, it's quite possible. Don't deny what your eyes can see, Maeve. You're an expert, are you not? You can see the age of the text; the damage that it has sustained. The ancient Latin and thoughtful stroke of the author's pen. And your reasoning mind knows that the museum would have authenticated anything that I put on loan to them; otherwise, they wouldn't be able to ever put it on display."

He took another drag on his cigarette.

Sebastian was right. Her reasoning mind did know all of these things. There was no doubt in her mind that the little piece of parchment was anything but authentic. She set down the magnifying glass and closed her eyes.

Immediately, her mind travelled to the Libre Vitae in the safe at the Bates Library for International Study back in New York City. The codex Sebastian had asked for her help in decoding. The Ottoman era clay tablet that was still in the safe at Shepheard's Hotel. All of these ancient texts from all over the world had one thing in common. And now sitting in front of her in a little cafe in Luxor, Egypt was another piece of the greater puzzle. Conveniently dated from the time after Jesus was resurrected from the dead in 33AD.

She had wrongly believed that the world's fascination with immortality was about living forever and avoiding death. But now she saw how erroneous she had been in that assumption. It wasn't about never dying—because bodies wore out after all.

As the text before her clearly stated. Immortality was about the essence of self. And the essence of self was the soul.

She opened her eyes as her brain clicked certain pieces of information into place. Sebastian was smiling at her now as if he could follow her thought process simply from her facial expressions. Maybe he could. The answer had finally dawned on her. If one could figure out how to preserve the soul indefinitely on the earth plane, then theoretically one could also live forever. Bodies may come and go, but the energetic makeup of the soul could go on indefinitely. Albert Einstein was the one who had pointed out that energy could neither be created nor destroyed. But that it could be transformed.

Her rational mind voiced the thought that her imagination did not want to give voice to: Transformed into what?

2092
NEW YORK CITY, UNITED STATES

A knock on the door of her office nearly scared Maeve out of her wits. She had been so focused on what she had just witnessed on the street below that she felt as though she were having an out of body experience.

Marco had definitely been there. And then he had clearly *not* been there.

She adamantly shook her head, sending tendrils of dark hair falling out of her ponytail. Since her office was small, she reached the door in two strides and pulled it open.

And for the second time in as many minutes, she nearly fell over with disbelief.

Standing in front of her was Marco.

Except he wasn't wearing the drab cashmere scarf she had gotten him for Christmas, nor was he wearing his wool coat. He appeared to be covered in a fine layer of dust that speckled his besweatered shoulders and his mousy brown hair.

She had stumbled back with surprise and Marco had grabbed her elbow to keep her upright. Now he entered her office and slowly moved Maeve toward one of the chairs by the window.

"Are you feeling alright? You look like you've seen a ghost."

As she lowered herself into the chair, she glanced at the hand holding her arm. Marco's sweater was pushed up to his elbows and his wrist was adorned with the strange watch. It was large but the face appeared black. What kind of watch had a black shiny face with no numbers?

She recovered quickly from her initial shock. "I'm fine." She gestured to her notebook and the scroll spread out on her small desk. "I was just lost in thought that's all."

Marco looked relieved, his dark brows relaxing. "Oh, that's good then."

"Why do you look like you were crawling around in some dark, dirty hole in the ground?" she asked inspecting him.

He shook his hair and sent particles of dust flying around her office. Maeve bit her lip in consternation.

"Because I was. Obviously. I came up here to see if you could give me a hand."

"Of course." She rolled up the codex and gathered her notebook and placed both items in the small safe hidden within the narrow bookshelf on her wall. Then she followed Marco out into the hallway.

"Are you sure you're alright? I've never seen you go so pale before."

The possibility of simply asking Marco to verify what she had seen did occur to her, but she didn't think it was worth the risk of him thinking she was mentally unstable or worse experiencing hallucinations. *No,* she decided, *it was best to act as normal as possible.* For now.

"Truthfully, I was just focused intently on my work and your knock startled me. I shouldn't let myself get so overly absorbed like that."

He looked at her curiously, but didn't ask her again. She followed him into the dumbwaiter and he hit the button to go back down. As the dumbwaiter rattled noisily, Maeve noticed that they were passing the basement level where Marco's office was located and where they typically sorted deliveries and that the dumbwaiter wasn't slowing down.

Noticing her confusion, Marco endeavored to explain. "The library has three lower levels. There's the street level, the basement just below that level where you and I usually work. Then there's the sub-basement and below that the sub-sub-basement. That's where we're headed."

"Why on earth would a building need three basements?" she asked.

"I thought you knew that the library was built on top of a previous structure?" Indeed, she had known that. But only because everything in the city was built on top of a pre-existing structure because the Third World War had decimated everything above ground. To save on both the time and cost of rebuilding once the nuclear fallout had cleared, many new builders had simply re-used existing substructures.

New York was even more fascinating in that many of the substructures were connected by an intricate tunnel system. She also knew that this was not unique to only New York City, but was actually the case in cities all over the world.

"I did know that," she replied. "However, I didn't realize that the existing substructure had three levels. Seems like overkill, doesn't it?"

The dumbwaiter came to a stop and Marco pushed the metal grate aside and chivalrously let Maeve exit first.

"The lower levels, like this one, are even older than the first basement level. It seems that this particular spot was built upon several times."

"Does that make this spot significant in some way?" Maeve asked.

"Perhaps," he replied ambiguously. Then he added, "It's difficult to guess anyone's reasoning without the proper context."

Maeve nodded but she had the feeling that he was purposefully omitting something from her.

She followed him down the hallway. The walls were cinder block and the floor was compacted dirt and it smelled dank and musty. Certainly, no artifacts or texts could be stored in such a humid environment.

The scant lighting cast eerie shadows as they walked and Maeve could hear the faint dripping of water in the distance. Just how far under the surface level were they?

Eventually, the corridor curved to the left and intuitively Maeve knew that they were heading in the direction of the park that was across the street from the library. After the curve, the corridor narrowed further before it came to a dead end at a large wooden door with iron hinges.

Marco had used a stone that had fallen out of the wall nearby to prop open the door. Maeve could feel a cold draft coming out of the narrow opening. If her interest hadn't been piqued before, now it was really and truly piqued.

He pulled the door with a theatric heave and the opening became wide enough for Maeve to pass through. Marco followed her and stood closely behind; she could feel his breath on the back of her neck.

Lit torches lined two of the walls on either side. The overall chamber was a square and the floor was laid with reddish brick as were the walls. There were arched alcoves among the walls. Several contained wooden shelves with metal boxes on them. One alcove without shelving contained a medieval looking suit of armor displayed within it, except it wasn't in great condition, with visible rust at various joints. Another alcove had a large flag bearing a crest Maeve had never seen before: it was a shield broken into four parts. The upper left contained a crocodile, the upper right had a cross in the Templar style, the bottom left had a sun with rays pointing out, and the lower right had a chalice. Even from across the room she could see that it was embroidered. The thread was gold on a rich navy background and the bottom of the flag had knotted golden tassels.

What really confused her though was that in front of them across from the door was a large stone altar. It had a base on either side that looked to be about two feet by two feet and there was a single slab of uncut stone across the top. She'd never seen anything like it. She stepped closer, out of the protective space of Marco behind her and inspected the altar.

She walked around it. Looked beneath it. And examined the top. Behind it in the wall at about eye-level was a smaller alcove than the others. It had a stone ledge that held a pack of long matches, a ceramic jug that reminded her of the vessels used for wine or oil in ancient Rome and Egypt, and a trio of small golden bowls. Maeve didn't have to touch them to know that they were made from actual gold, not simply gilded. Laying across the ledge was a long narrow knife. Its blade looked to be obsidian and the handle was wood, but wrapped with worn leather cord.

After her inspection she turned to Marco who was still standing by the door and hadn't yet moved. He had simply watched her as she progressed around the chamber. Various questions swirled in her mind. What was Marco doing down here anyways? How did he find this room? Was he the one who lit the torches or had they already been lit? But the most important question was the one she voiced first.

"What is this place?" she asked.

The flame from the torches cast his pale face in odd shadows and made his cheeks look gaunt and his eyes like hollowed out dark sockets.

"I was hoping that you could tell me."

2101
UNDISCLOSED LOCATION, SWITZERLAND

The scientist had been given her instructions, but she wasn't sure she liked them. She stood alone in her lab with her arms crossed. It was midnight and everyone was gone. There was no chance she would be interrupted. Part of her wished someone would come barging into the lab and interrupt this madness.

That's what it was: madness!

She sat down on the rolling stool and pushed herself to the stainless-steel countertop. She slipped on a pair of nitrile gloves resigned to the fact that she couldn't procrastinate much longer. They had given her a deadline and she had to get moving.

Naturally, she didn't know who exactly the deadline came from. A container marked hazardous materials had shown up at the lab with her name on it, which wasn't all that unusual. What was unusual was that she also had received a letter within minutes of its arrival that provided her very specific instructions on what to do with the material and where to send it after she had completed the instructions. There had been no return address and the letter had been typed on a typewriter.

She could have ignored the package and the letter, but something deep inside her had told her that would be a very bad idea. That something, she had come to realize, was a very primal urge for self-preservation. She would do as the letter instructed and then wash her hands of the whole affair.

Her microscope was already set up and she moved the glass jar closer. She removed the lid, briefly inhaling the familiar scent of formaldehyde. Using tongs, she carefully removed the object suspended in the colorless liquid of preservation. She carefully placed the object on a stainless-steel tray and switched out her tongs for a scalpel.

The object was fleshy yet firm beneath her fingertips. It was roughly the size of a ping-pong ball. Using the scalpel she carefully scraped away a thin film of tissue. If she did it right the first time that would be all that she needed. Carefully she slid the gel-like slimy tissue into a small glass dish.

Then she sat down her scalpel and picked up the tongs again to place the eyeball back into the glass jar of formaldehyde. She tightened its lid and moved onto the next object that had been in the strange package she had received.

She pulled out a small glass vial with a dropper located inside its lid. The oleaginous substance was ruby red and glittered in the light. She uncapped it and drew some of the liquid up into the dropper then carefully deposited three drops into the petri dish along with her freshly collected human cells. Her eyes grew wide in surprise as the droplets appeared to ball up and separate from one another then hop around the dish as if of their own accord.

They danced around and seemed as though they were inspecting the thin sample of tissue. Then in perfect orchestration they merged together and seemed to leap into the tissue. Immediately the tissue began to seize and turned the same ruby red as the mysterious liquid. She recapped the vial and watched in amazement as the tissue began to incrementally increase in size.

Nervously, she glanced back at the instructions. Shrugging her shoulders she picked up the glass dish and placed it at the bottom of what was essentially a six-foot glass incubator. Typically, it was used in experiments with plants, but the instructions had explicitly said that's where the specimen should be placed. She closed the incubator and locked the door.

She began packing up the box. The final instruction was to send the box back. The address didn't give her any additional clues. It was in the United States, but she'd never heard of the city although it was located in Alaska. There was no street address just a post office box number.

Once the box was repackaged, she tossed her gloves into a hazardous waste basket and then washed her hands thoroughly. She removed her white lab coat and switched it for her rain slicker. Grabbing her umbrella and the box, she gave the room a final look before she closed the door behind her. Her footsteps echoed down the hallway.

She had already hailed herself a cab, so she didn't hear the crash when the glass dish inside the incubator fell to the floor. And she was nearly all the way home when a ping-pong ball sized eyeball with a brown iris rolled out of the substance within the dish and looked wildly around the glass chamber in which it was now trapped.

2079
LUXOR, EGYPT

Maeve and Sebastian had passed the brunt of the afternoon sun sitting in the shade of the restaurant. Now they were walking down the winding cobbled streets. Vendors were resuming their places for the late afternoon and early evening influx of tourists, who all had scuttled back to their hotels for luncheon and to pass the time until the hottest part of the day had subsided.

Shop owners called out to them offering the best deals on their wares for the "lovely American Sitt!" She wondered if they thought Sebastian was a native because of his darkly tanned skin and jet-black wavy hair. He did indulge one vendor and presented her with a pretty bouquet of marigolds that were a fluffy and vibrant yellow.

As she happily walked beside Sebastian with his hand in hers, she wondered how she could ever leave. She hadn't been this happy in a very long time. Thinking back to the last time she had been this happy, it was also with Sebastian. The first two years of their relationship had been both an intellectual and romantic whirlwind. One particular event snuck back into her consciousness and she adamantly stuffed it back in its mental box and pushed it into a dark, cobwebby corner. She would not let anything distract her from this moment.

She brought herself back to the present.

"It's just this way," Sebastian was saying as he tugged her along.

Suddenly, she felt a woosh of air past her right ear. Instinctively, she leaped forward and tackled Sebastian from behind sending the beautiful flowers flying through the air. The movement sent him sprawling to the cobblestones face down with her landing across his back. Her satchel containing the shoe box with the ancient religious text was sandwiched in between them painfully digging into her rib cage.

Sebastian said something but she couldn't make it out since his mouth was muffled against the stones. Vendors, shoppers, and passerby had gathered around them inadvertently encircling them in a protective barrier.

Maeve knew they must have looked ridiculous but she didn't care as she rolled off Sebastian's back and knelt beside him still clutching the satchel. The crowd murmured as Sebastian rolled onto his back and looked heavenward. The fall had scraped his cheek and chin. The leg of his trousers was torn around the knee, but otherwise he appeared to be okay, although his eyes were still closed.

"Sebastian," Maeve whispered. He held up a hand and she realized that when she tackled him, she had knocked the breath straight out of him.

A tall man with curly blonde hair, blue eyes, and a neatly trimmed mustache and beard stepped forward. He was wearing a straw boating hat and dressed in a tan linen suit with espadrille loafers.

"I am a doctor," he explained. The way he pronounced doctor sounded more like *doktor* with heavy emphasis on the first syllable. To Maeve's trained ears and the man's somewhat traditional appearance, she deduced that there was a high probability that the doctor was German.

At the man's words Sebastian sat up. "*Mir geht es gut, Doktor.* " Maeve grabbed one of his arms and the doctor grabbed the other and they helped Sebastian to his feet. "Truly, I am fine. Just needed a minute because *meine liebe Freundin* knocked the wind out of me."

"I, uh, tripped. On a loose cobblestone, I think." Maeve knew she was a horrible liar; she was much better at lying by omission, so she tried to look abashed to compensate.

The doctor smiled. "That was quite a feat of athleticism."

Now Maeve flushed at the compliment. She had acted without thinking, it was her natural instinct to protect Sebastian. Always.

A young Arab boy stepped forward out of the crowd which had already grown bored with the situation and had begun to disperse. He stepped up to Sebastian with his arm outstretched and a lopsided grin on his face. "It was this, Effendi."

Sebastian held out his palm and the young lad dropped something into it. Sebastian's fingers curled around the object and with his other hand, Sebastian reached into his pocket and dropped some coins into the boy's hand as thanks. The grin widened and the boy darted away and disappeared down one of the many alleys.

Maeve glanced over Sebastian's shoulder as he uncurled his fingers. It was made of papyrus reed and sharpened to a point. The point had a bunch of cotton fibers at the end.

The dart itself would do little damage. It was what the dart had been soaked in which Maeve had no doubt was some kind of poison, but there was no way to tell without a chemical analysis. The usual was some kind of natural poison from the sap of a tree or vine, for example the South American curare poison that would cause paralysis. Paralysis included the respiratory muscles and eventually would lead to suffocation, at least in animals. To kill a full-sized adult, there would likely need to be several darts.

The doctor leaned over Sebastian's other shoulder. "Peculiar that, *nein*?"

Sebastian glowered at his hand. "Quite." He encircled the dart in his fist and discarded the item into his pocket.

"You're sure you're alright, young man? This woman may have saved you from a very unpleasant experience."

Now Sebastian's glower softened as he looked at Maeve. "Indeed. Nor would it be the first or last time that has she done so." He reached out and squeezed her hand. "And, yes *doktor*. I'm sure I'm fine. Just a few scrapes and bruises from my fall."

"Ah, then we shall part ways." He fumbled around in his suit pockets until he produced a small card and handed it to Sebastian. "In case you should be in need of my services. *Bis*

Bald. Goodbye for now." He tipped his hat to them and walked away in the general direction of the temples and ruins.

Sebastian flipped the card in his fingers and lifted it so they both could read it.

Dr. Theobald H. Schmidt, MD with a phone number and an office location in Cairo.

He slipped the card into his pocket and his eyes scanned the area. Maeve followed his gaze. She knew that he was looking for where the assailant could have been located. She noticed a tenant building behind them only about a hundred feet from where they had been. That could be a possibility if their assailant had been local, or if they had not been local and were criminally minded, they could have simply broken into an apartment. Her eyes moved to the right and she noticed a cluster of palm trees. The assailant could have climbed one and shot the dart from there. She narrowed her eyes, but didn't notice anything peculiar or even any movement. The afternoon was not generous with a breeze.

Sebastian must have concluded the same things as her, so he turned and they walked close to the façade of the building beneath the awning. His pace was quick and he turned down the first alley on their right. He startled her when he stopped and pushed her against the wall—she thought he had seen something farther up the alley, but relief flooded her when he kissed her. His hand let go of hers and found her face.

When he stopped, she gave him a quizzical look. As much as she had enjoyed the interlude, this neither seemed the time nor the place.

"You keep saving my life," he said. His face was still very close to hers because he hadn't pulled away. She noticed that one of the cuts on his chin was still bleeding and that above his right eye a bruise was forming. She really had tackled him hard and was relieved she hadn't broken his nose. He must have turned his face slightly to the left before he hit the ground.

"I wouldn't have to keep saving it if you didn't keep putting it in danger," she pointed out.

He laughed, finally pulling away and continuing down the alley. As her heartbeat calmed down, she caught up to him and looped her arm through his.

"Do you think it has anything to do with the Gaul text?" she asked in a low voice. There was no one else in the alley with them, but she didn't want to take any chances that they could be heard.

"It's hard to say. It could be. Then again, it could be the same assailant from before and they think we are still walking around with the clay tablet."

She gave voice to a thought she didn't really want to. "What if it's two different assailants?"

Sebastian was quiet for a moment. "Then we need to start being very careful."

They walked in silence after that. Ludwig's wasn't all that far from where the attack had occurred. The bottom floor of the building was a rug shop with beautiful Persian rugs with vibrant colors. Many hung from the shops rafters and others were rolled on tables. An older man with a long white beard sat on a stool smoking a pipe. He nodded at Sebastian as they passed. A set of metal stairs to the left of the building took them up to the second floor. There was only one door and it was painted what once had likely been a cheerful shade of red, but which was now chipped and peeling.

Sebastian knocked and then after a couple of minutes knocked again. At this second attempt there came what sounded like the banging of pots from behind the door. The door was yanked open so hard that Sebastian reached out to grab Maeve before she tumbled back down the steps. There really wasn't enough room for two people on the little landing.

Ludwig was not what she expected. Sebastian had mentioned he was a German ex-pat who had suffered an accident on one of his archaeological digs, thus ending his career. Because of this she had made the assumption that Ludwig would be old. This assumption turned out to be erroneous.

From his face he appeared to be in his thirties—closer to Maeve's age in this time period—but the full head of long white hair was deceiving. Upon closer inspection Maeve noticed the white was actually the palest shade of blonde she had ever seen. His eyes were an ambiguous shade of hazel and they regarded them through the open door with what Maeve considered a glare. She did not find it all that intimidating because the top of the man's head came up to about her collarbone which meant he was nearly a full foot shorter than Sebastian.

When his glance went from Maeve—who he had clearly discerned as an interruption—to Sebastian his face broke out into a smile. He grabbed Sebastian's hand and shook it vigorously, pumping it up and down with so much force his entire body moved.

"Come in! Come in! Old friend!" Everything he said sounded as if it was punctuated with exclamation points.

Sebastian nudged Maeve ahead of him so that she followed Ludwig into his apartment. It took up the entire second floor of the rug shop below. She wondered if he rented it from the rug shop owner. It was set up studio style with a kitchenette down the right side of the apartment with a well-used dining set with two chairs being closest to the door. Even from the entryway, Maeve could see that the sink was piled high with dishes and that there was a large pot on the stove that appeared to be boiling over and water hissed as it hit the stove top.

To the immediate left was a large sofa that was green with thin burgundy stripes. One of the cushions had been torn and batting spilled onto the worn wooden floor. In the far-left corner was a bed which consisted of a mattress on the floor. There were only two windows in the place. One on the kitchenette side that looked out the front of the building and onto the street below and one on the opposite wall near the bed that had the most beautiful view of palm trees swaying against a cloudless blue sky. Directly across from Maeve was a door that she guessed led to a privy of some kind. From wall to wall she could take in the entire space from where she stood at the door.

"Can I get you something! Tea! Coffee!" Ludwig asked turning to Maeve. "And your lovely friend, Sebastain, you rascal!"

"Ludwig, this is Maeve. She is also a scholar of antiquities. Maeve, this is Ludwig." He stepped in and closed the door behind him.

Before she could reply, Ludwig grasped her hand and enthusiastically began shaking it as he had Sebastian's. A pair of spectacles had been perched on the top of his head and now they were hanging precariously from his left ear.

"I think you have something boiling over on the stove," was all that Maeve could manage.

Ludwig dropped her hand and turned toward the kitchen with a look of surprise on his face. As the water began to boil over in earnest he hurried over and removed it from the burner. Luckily, he remembered to turn it off.

"I wonder what I was making!" she heard him mumble to himself. He placed the pot in the sink and shrugged before turning back to them.

"Come! Come! Sit!" He gestured to the little wooden table and its two chairs.

Sebastian leaned in close to her ear. "Don't worry, he's so jittery he won't sit down."

Maeve took the chair closer to the window and Sebastian the other.

"Are you sure I can't get you anything!" Ludwig asked.

"Just some water would be lovely, old pal," Sebastian said with a smile.

Maeve watched as he pulled two cups from one of the cabinets and filled them with water. She hoped they were clean, although she'd probably had worse come to think of it. The little apartment was warm and the window was closed. Ludwig was wearing an ivory knit sweater which Maeve wasn't sure why someone living in the dessert would even own a knit sweater.

Ludwig brought over the two cups and sat them down on the table, then noticing his spectacles just before they fell off his ear and onto the table, he caught them and placed them on his face. They magnified his hazel eyes so that he looked bug-eyed.

Sebastian took a sip without a second thought, so Maeve figured it was probably alright to drink. After he had refreshed himself, he addressed Ludwig.

"My friend, I received your message while I was in Cairo. I apologize for the delay in my arrival. We had encountered a couple of…difficulties."

Maeve almost snorted water out of her nose. If you could call being almost murdered two different times a difficulty.

Ludwig glanced at her curiously, but Sebastian ignored her.

"Your message indicated that you had acquired something that you wanted to show me? I also have something I'd like to show you."

Ludwig had begun pacing from the bed to the table and back again. As he did so he wringed his hands. Maeve felt sad for whatever injuries he had suffered from his archaeological accident. It appeared to have made him rather scatter-brained and wrought with anxiety.

"Yes, yes! It's here somewhere!"

Between the mattress and the bathroom door there was a wide bookcase. It was overflowing with boxes and books and half-drunk cups of tea. For the first time she noticed an orange brindled cat curled up on the very top shelf fast asleep, its tail draped over the front of the bookcase in a sleepy J.

Ludwig went to the book case and began scanning it mumbling to himself as he went.

Sebastian watched on with a placid expression and sipped at his water. His hands tapped on his cigarette case that rested in his shirt pocket now, but he was too polite to even ask Ludwig if he could smoke.

It was for the better. The apartment was downright stuffy and she wondered why Ludwig had all the windows closed. Up here she'd think there'd be a rather pleasant cross breeze if he opened both windows on either side.

Ludwig had made several false pronouncements that he'd found what he was looking for only to recant and continue searching. The apartment wasn't all that large, untidy yes, but there were only so many places for an object to go and aside from the bathroom, one could see them all.

Maeve took the interlude to study Sebastian's face as he watched the eccentric archaeologist. His cut had stopped bleeding, but it was still a bright red and the bruise on the right side of his face was turning a plum shade of purple. His lips were quirked up to one side in a half smile and his blue eyes were amused as he followed the little man back and forth along the bookcase.

Her eyes moved down to his tanned neck. His crocodile pendent was still there, but looked like it had jammed into his neck when he hit the ground and left an oddly shaped red mark. One of the buttons on his shirt was missing as well.

"Do I pass?" he asked interrupting her study.

She started to roll her eyes, but when they returned to his face his expression had changed. Before she could retort something witty, Ludwig cried out.

"I found it! It's always in the last place you look!"

He rushed over to them tripping over his own feet in his excitement. In his hands was a small book. It looked like a journal of some kind complete with a brass latch containing a keyhole. Luckily, the little book wasn't locked because finding the key would have been a whole other ordeal, of that Maeve was certain.

When he placed the book on the table, Sebastian set his water glass off to the side. It was a deep worn brown leather, well-oiled from hands over the years. Even just looking at it, Maeve could tell that it was very old. Some of the binding was frayed and the edges of the pages were yellowed like tea. It was rather thick, but the cover of the book didn't give any indication of its contents or owners. It was smooth and plain.

Sebastian ran a finger across the cover and tapped it.

"This isn't what I think it is, is it?" he asked.

Maeve asked, "What is it that you think it is?"

Ludwig was outright beaming and it changed his entire countenance. She could see the excited young archaeologist he had once been.

"It's a journal that once belonged to the most well-known alchemist in the world!"

"Surely not—" Maeve began, but Ludwig's enthusiasm was contagious.

Sebastian emphatically tapped the cover again and his face was alight with excitement. "This is the journal of Nicholas Flamel!"

1483 AD
PARIS, FRANCE

A young man with flaming red hair entered the bookshop. The bookseller looked up when the small bell above the door rang to let him know that someone had entered. The young man was dressed in a black wool tunic covered with a thick wool doublet in an austere shade of gray. His ginger-colored hair stuck out from beneath a black wool beret and his knee-high black leather boots were polished to a shine.

He strode into the shop as if he owned the place, which he did not. The bookseller quietly observed him from his spot on a wooden stool behind the counter at the back of the shop. He couldn't see in between the rows of wooden shelves from there, but he could see down the main aisle that led from the door to the counter. This man was not here to browse.

As if he could read the bookseller's mind, the man strode down the middle aisle and straight to the back counter. The old man did not rise. His ankles and knees were arthritic and it made it painful to rise quickly from a prolonged seated position, as he had been all morning and well into the afternoon because he had been waiting somewhat impatiently for the younger man to arrive.

When he got a good look at him and the air of wealth that permeated his being, the older man was not surprised. These young nobles thought the entire world could wait for them. Indeed, for the right price it could.

In a show of respect, the ginger-haired man removed his beret. His hair shone in the candlelight of the shop as if it were a copper denier newly minted.

He bowed slightly toward the old man. Even that simple gesture was regal. "Nicholas Flamel, I presume."

The old man nodded as the younger straightened. "You presume correctly."

While the lad had a pompous air about him, his green eyes were bright with curiosity. The spattering of freckles across his nose and cheeks further indicated just how youthful the man truly was.

The younger clutched his beret and implored the elder.

"I have heard many great things about you, *Monsieur Flamel*. I am hoping that you can help me."

For the right price, the old man thought.

"What is it that you think an old man like me could help you with?"

The man's face took on a mischievous gleam. "I know you are much, much older than you appear. It is said that you carry the age of those of the Biblia Sacra."

Nicholas couldn't help himself. He snorted, but quickly turned it into a cough. "Not the 969 years of Methuselah."

"You were born in 1330, *ce n'est pas vrai?*"

He had to give the lad credit. He certainly had done his research. Nicholas appreciated that. Most of the nobles who crossed his path were vain fools. Better to be a vain man of intelligence at least.

"*C'est vrai,*" Nicholas replied. "What exactly is it that you think I can do? I am but a humble bookseller." He expected the usual response when he asked this question. *I want you to make me young forever. I want you to make me invincible. I want you to help me escape death.*

Unfortunately, he could not help with any of these things. Age was a biological process, and while it could be slowed and prolonged, it could not be completely halted. Invincibility was another thing altogether. He could not make bone turn into metal or a fatal wound to heal. And only God could stop death.

"*Je veux vivre éternellement.*" The young man's eyes were alight and his hands shook ever so slightly. "It is rumored that you are an alchemist. A very, very good alchemist. I have much money."

As if to prove his point he dropped his beret onto the counter and reached into his cloak and removed two large velvet sacks that clanked and jingled when he placed them on the counter in front of Nicholas.

He wearily regarded the sacks.

"It will not make you young forever, nor will it render you invincible…" This was usually his last attempt to dissuade someone from his services. He felt he at least owed them that due diligence.

"*Oui, oui, mais bien sûr,*" the young man acceded. "I only want to be assured a long life."

It was a simple enough request. And looking at the sacks of money, the young nobleman was happy to pay handsomely for Nicholas's services. For a normal man, it would be a question of conscience. One could not escape death, not truly. Oh, you could try to outrun it for a while, but it would always catch up to you. And sometimes, as he had seen firsthand, with a vengeance.

Nicholas slid the sacks of money off the countertop and directly into a trunk below the counter.

Luckily, he was not a normal man. Conscience was of little concern to him.

2092
NEW YORK CITY, UNITED STATES

Maeve knew that the thing that should have disturbed her the most about the hidden room should have been the altar. But that wasn't the thing that continued to nag at her a month later.

She had feinted Marco's question with a shrug. How could she possibly know what the place was used for? Obviously, she could deduce all the same things that he did. That it was a meeting place of some kind, likely ceremonial in nature. But for how long had it been there and for whose use? Just because it was accessible through the library didn't implicate Sebastian. When she had said this Marco's brown eyes had narrowed considerably and she recalled that strange day in the park when he had tried to warn her off growing closer to Sebastian.

Feeling defensive, she'd elaborated that there was an entire network of tunnels under the entire city so theoretically, unless the tunnels were blocked off, the room could be accessible by anyone.

Marco had begrudgingly conceded defeat, at least temporarily. She wasn't sure why he'd wanted to even show her the room in the first place, unless he was hoping that she could somehow implicate Sebastian. But implicate him in what? And who exactly *was* Marco anyways? Obviously, he was not just an innocent little book clerk. She liked him well enough, but she knew what she had witnessed was impossible. She needed to catch him in the act of disappearing out of thin air. Yes, she would have to confront him sooner or later.

However, right now she had more pressing things to think about, so she shoved those thoughts aside to be addressed at a later time. The thing that had kept nagging at her was the flag.

The crest had contained a crocodile, a cross in the Knights Templar style with the flourish on the ends, a sun with rays pointing out—drawn like spokes—and a chalice. It was an odd array of images and rich with symbolism. But what could it mean? Did it belong to some secret organization? A secret society of some kind?

Her head was spinning with thoughts, so she pulled out her notebook and made a little table with the symbols drawn on the left-hand side as best she could replicate them, and a section to the right headed with the words: meaning/relevance.

The cross was easiest for her as the straightforward meanings were clear, at least from a historical perspective. The Templars were basically the bank of the early Church. They also supposedly were responsible for protecting various holy relics. They also were all burned at the stake after a decree by Clement the V in 1307.

A chalice coincided nicely with the Templar symbolism. The simplest explanation was that a chalice was a drinking vessel. However, her historical knowledge knew that it was much more than that. She'd read stories about the Holy Grail, supposedly the chalice used by Jesus at the Last Supper. That would have been a holy relic under the Knights Templar jurisdiction. Chalices were also commonly bejeweled and decorated during the medieval era. Some were works of art in their own right.

The other two symbols puzzled her a bit more in juxtaposition to the cross and chalice. She knew from Sebastian's love of Egyptian history that the heretic pharaoh Akhenaton had tried to convert Egypt to monotheism, worshipping what he believed to be the one true god, Aten — or an aspect of the sun god Re (also sometimes Ra). Needless to say, this decision didn't go over well with the polytheistic pagan citizens of his kingdom. The reason the sun was worshipped by many ancient cultures was because it was synonymous with life.

All that was left then was the crocodile. Since the right side of the crest seemed related to medieval Christian symbolism, she wondered if logic could follow that the left-hand side was related to Egyptian symbolism. If that was the case she would need to do more research. All she knew off-hand was that the ancient Egyptians believed certain animals were associated with different things like fertility, protection, beauty, or wealth. She drew a circle around the word crocodile.

Satisfied that was as far as she was likely to get for now without further research, she placed her pencil in her notebook to mark the page and closed it. The day was bright and sunny. It was still spring, but summer was itching to make an appearance. The past week had been rainy and instead of sitting in her office on this bright day, she decided she should be outside enjoying the reprieve from rain.

As if reading her mind, at that moment there was a knock on her office door. She went and opened it and was surprised to see Sebastian standing there. He was still in his travelling coat and a plaid scarf was draped loosely around his neck. Clearly, he had come straight from the train station. His eyes lit up when he saw her and she let him swoop her up and into his arms.

He kissed her enthusiastically and mumbled into her neck. "It's been too long. I think I am going to have to start taking you with me on these trips."

She pulled back and regarded him. "Business or pleasure."

His smile widened. "Can it not be both?"

She pulled him into her office and closed the door behind him. He removed his coat and draped it over the back of one of the chairs. Her office was quaint compared to his which had a homey feel like his reading room which was often her preferred place to work, but as their relationship had deepened, she didn't want to give an opportunity for Marco or anyone else to call into question her qualifications. Sebastian had resisted at first, but she had won the argument and Sebastian had arranged for the tiny space in which they now stood to become her office.

Once his coat was removed, she saw the flash of jewels at his wrist and realized he was wearing the odd watch she had seen accompanied by the peculiar note. She hadn't thought about it since she'd seen it and a strange feeling of foreboding came over her.

She stepped toward him and wrapped her arms around his waist. He'd been gone for three weeks this time. He kissed the top of her head and glanced at her notebook.

"Did I interrupt your work?"

She could tell from the hopeful note in his voice that he'd hoped she'd been working on the codex. She felt a twinge of guilt that she had been working on something that had nothing to do with any of her assignments and more than likely had something to do with Marco's strange caution against Sebastian.

She decided it was probably worth a subtle attempt to try and find out what Sebastian knew about the tunnels beneath the library.

"No, you didn't interrupt me. I needed a break from the codex. You know that I'm not particularly fond of numbers. I have made a little headway, but truthfully, I think that we need an expert."

He sat in the chair and pulled her onto his lap. "You are an expert, my darling."

"You know what I mean. Someone who is known for codebreaking. I'm sure of all your acquaintances around the world, there is someone you would be willing to take into your confidence?"

"Hmm. Maybe," he conceded. "What else have you been up to while I've been away?"

"I did do a little exploring," she admitted.

"Exploring, eh?" he asked and kissed her again. When he was finished, he continued. "I enjoy exploring. Did I mention that three weeks is too long?"

"You did," she laughed, but refused to be distracted as much as she enjoyed Sebastian's attempts. She continued, "I meant exploring in the library. Did you know that the library sits above the tunnel system?"

"Actually, I did know that. It runs for miles and miles beneath the city and beyond. Darling, you shouldn't go exploring down there. It could be dangerous. Since they've been abandoned, sections have become unstable and some tunnels have even collapsed. Besides, what were you even doing on the lower levels?"

"I was just curious. I'd never realized there were additional levels beyond the storage level. Are you certain that all of the tunnels have been abandoned? It would be quite the place for a secretive gathering or for someone to hide things that they didn't want to be found."

Sebastian looked thoughtful. "I agree with you that it would be a wonderful spot for a secret society to meet and conduct their secret rituals."

His face was serious when he spoke and she wondered if he knew exactly what she was referring to until he added, "But I assure you they've been abandoned since the post-war period. Like I already said, it's very dangerous. Only a fool would mess around in those tunnels."

When she looked into the deep blue of his eyes, she knew that he was telling the truth. But if he wasn't the one using the tunnels, then who was?

He pulled her closer and kissed her again. "Did I mention three weeks was too long?"

She smiled against his lips deciding to allow herself to get lost in the moment for the time being. Besides, she could think about tunnels, Egyptian symbolism, and secret societies later.

"Once or twice."

2079
LUXOR, EGYPT

"Isn't Nicholas Flamel a fictionalized character?" Maeve asked doubtfully.

"Oh, no, my dear!" Ludwig exclaimed (this time the exclamation was appropriate). "He was very much a real person!"

Sebastian interjected. "Records show that he was alive during the Middle Ages in France. Not only was he a scribe and a bookseller, but he and his wife funded many schools with their vast wealth."

Maeve couldn't help thinking of the various fictionalized versions of Nicholas Flamel. "So, he wasn't an alchemist?"

"Oh, no, he was definitely an alchemist!" Sebastian laughed. "And quite a good one at that. While some historians and authors may have gotten carried away with the whole philosopher's stone bit, that doesn't mean that there wasn't any actual science involved."

"His discoveries enabled him to live to be one-hundred-and-fifty-three years old! Although history would have you believe he died at the age of eighty-eight!" Ludwig chortled.

The journal was in remarkable condition if it was indeed from medieval times. She knew without asking that it was authentic. Sebastian wouldn't even entertain seeing something if the provenance didn't prove impeccable—at least her Sebastian from the present. Maybe the younger version of the man was less concerned about verifying an object's origins. But she thought it unlikely as she recalled Ami's impeccable provenance of the clay tablet.

He lifted the latch and carefully opened the book. Both Ludwig and Maeve leaned closer in anticipation. Naturally, it was in French which Maeve couldn't read, but she knew Sebastian could. With the beautiful calligraphy she noticed some Latin words mixed in which she was able to quickly translate. Words like immortality, alchemy, and equation. The pages were also filled with strange symbols the likes of which Maeve had never seen before.

Sebastian's brow furrowed as he glanced through the yellowed pages before abruptly closing the book. Maeve sensed it at the same time he did. A peculiar sensation that crept up her spine accompanied by a dire sense of foreboding. Call it a premonition or intuition, either way they had both felt it.

"You've done well, my friend." Sebastian nudged the book toward Maeve who obediently put it into her satchel which was now bulging with the two artifacts.

Ludwig leaned forward eagerly as Sebastian pulled a roll of money from the pocket of his pants and began counting out bills onto the table.

She saw Sebastian's eye twitch involuntarily and she knew that he had heard the same sound that she did—someone was coming up the stairs.

As Ludwig scooped up the money there was a pounding at the door and the sound of voices. Ludwig looked panicked for a moment as he shoved the money into a kettle. His hazel eyes still magnified behind his glasses were full of panic.

"I assume you weren't expecting additional visitors?" Sebastian asked.

Ludwig shook his head. "The window!" He pointed to the window facing the back of the building.

Sebastian stood and pulled Maeve to her feet and once again she found herself being dragged for a harrowing escape.

As Sebastian heaved the window open, Maeve looked back at Ludwig who stood wringing his hands by the door. The pounding and shouts—in German it sounded like—were growing louder and more insistent.

"We can't just leave him!" Maeve protested, gesturing toward Ludwig. Sebastian started to push her toward the now open window.

"It's not him that they want!" Sebastian lifted her up and placed her gently through the window. There was about a six-foot drop onto a flat roof. He lowered her carefully until her feet were just dangling and she was able to only drop the remaining foot or so. She saw Sebastian turn around presumably to say something to Ludwig, then he was out the window and just as his fingers released, the window slammed shut.

From the side of the building, she heard a crash. Sebastian grabbed her hand and they ran down the rooftop avoiding the fenestrations. When they reached the other side, there was a rusty metal ladder attached to the back of the building.

"I'll go first this time," Sebastian said and immediately climbed over the low parapet and began descending down the ladder. She hoped that Ludwig could hold off their pursuers long enough for them to get away and get lost.

She swung her leg over the parapet and began descending down the ladder after Sebastian. Her palms were sweaty and she kept losing her grip. What was it about these artifacts that their attackers wanted so badly? Why did they seem willing to kill to even get them?

Sebastian said something to her but she heard him too late as her foot lost purchase on a rusted out rung of the ladder. It was so unexpected she lost her grip, banging her chin on the rung near her face. She held on for dear life, not sure how close she was to the ground below.

Above her head she could hear the pounding of heavy steps and angry voices. She couldn't hang on indefinitely. She'd have to make a choice.

"Let go!" Sebastian called. He didn't sound all that far away. Realizing she needed reassurance, he added, "It's only a five-foot drop. I'll catch you."

Yeah, right, she thought. *And I'll squash you like a bug when I land on you.* But then he said the magic words.

"Trust me!"

That was all she needed to hear because she did trust Sebastian, more than anyone else and with every ounce of her being because never had he once given her reason not to trust him. No matter when or where in time, she trusted Sebastian with her life because she knew he valued her life as much as if not more than his own.

So, she let go of the death grip she had around the disintegrating metal ladder and let herself free fall right into Sebastian's waiting arms. He grunted and almost toppled over when he caught the force of her weight, but that slim, lithe form held her tight. Instinctively, she put her arms around his neck and finding her face so close to his she could have kissed him, but there wasn't any time.

Just as he set her down there was a shout from above them and the sound of gun fire. It sounded sporadic as if they didn't know exactly where their quarry was located. A bullet hit a bicycle near a tree and ricocheted.

Sebastian grabbed her hand and they stayed close to the building before reaching the corner.

There weren't many places to make a run for it. They could head out toward the desert but that seemed like a death sentence, or they could try and lose their pursuers among the tourists and try to make their way back to the hotel. Regardless they needed to get lost and fast.

In the distance, she could hear more angry shouts, but they seemed to be growing farther away as they broke into a run. They ran hard and in the direction of a small temple complex with an obelisk standing sentry. Sebastian was a swift and graceful runner. Maeve had sweat dripping into and burning her eyes and her heart felt like it was going to burst out of her chest and keep right on running. Just as her legs turned to a rubbery numbness, Sebastian led her straight into one of temples.

They ran through the rows upon rows of columns. Maeve's academic brain wished that they could stop because she'd never seen anything like the tall pillars with their carved hieroglyphics. She could easily get lost in this place and if their pursuers caught up to them, she hoped they would too. Sebastian however knew exactly where he was going. He zigged and zagged before finding a doorway and leading her out of the temple and back into the maze of streets behind the temple complex.

Breathing hard, Maeve leaned against the warm limestone of the building's façade. The streets were active with tourists now that the warmest part of the day had passed and the dinner hour would soon be approaching.

She glanced at Sebastian who barely had a hair on his pretty head out of place. She realized he had only stopped running to accommodate her. Embarrassed she asked, "Where should we go now?"

"We'll have to go back to the hotel. It's only a couple of blocks from here. I think it's the safest bet. They don't just let anyone storm into the Winter Palace. We'll be safe there, for now."

He took her hand and his pace was much slower.

Maeve took the reprieve to regroup her thoughts. Were the men who had banged on Ludwig's door the same as the men who had tried to incapacitate Sebastian with a blow dart? What about the men who had stabbed at them in Cairo? Had they been followed all this way? Or maybe it was an intricate gang of criminals? Her mission had taken a turn for the complicated. Naturally, when it came to Sebastian nothing was ever black and white.

And then a thought occurred to her that hadn't previously. Suppose it was a network of criminals; logic would assume they were after the artifacts because that's when the attacks had started. But there was also the minute possibility that they weren't after the artifacts. What if they were after Sebastian or Maeve herself?

Sebastian hadn't mentioned being pursued by anyone and she happened to show up just as he was acquiring more of these objects. The timing was strange and there was something about it that tickled at the back of her brain, but that she couldn't quite bring into focus.

They reached the hotel and Sebastian retrieved their key. He had his arm around her as he led her up the steps. They did get some strange looks, mainly because Sebastian was covered in dirt and dust and Maeve was sure she looked like a wreck between the sweat and the dirt—her face was probably still flushed from the exertion of all that running. She was also fairly certain that her chin had a cut on it from banging against the ladder rung. She noticed if Sebastian caught anyone's eye, he smiled winningly and the person immediately looked embarrassed and turned their attention away.

Finally, they reached their room.

Once inside, Sebastian released her, locked and bolted the door, and then dragged one of the beautifully upholstered chairs over and shoved it beneath the door knob. Then he went over to the windows and inspected them. They were on the third floor, so she felt it unlikely anyone could reach them. Still, Sebastian made sure that the windows were locked. There was no balcony so nobody could climb up that way either.

Satisfied, he flopped onto the divan and ran a hand over his face.

"We should clean up," Maeve said. "Then figure out a plan."

Without uncovering his face, Sebastian agreed with her. "You go on ahead. I need to think for a minute."

She left her satchel on the floor beside the divan in case Sebastian wanted to look over the scroll or the journal and made her way into the bath chamber. She only had a couple of changes of clothes; she'd need to put a ticket into the hotel laundry.

Her muscles already ached and the hot water from the shower felt divine. She also noticed she had a lot more bruises than she recalled having before this trip. Just because it didn't hurt, didn't mean that it didn't leave a mark. She couldn't even account for half of them.

Not bothering to dry her hair, she twisted it up into a bun and slipped into a pleasant pink linen button down and a pair of narrow cut twill pants. It wasn't her first choice, but when the agency did the packing, you got whatever they thought you would need.

When she reappeared Sebastian had sat up and was intently studying the journal of Nicholas Flamel. She already knew that Sebastian was fluent in French and that he could easily translate Latin, in addition to being able to speak and read numerous other languages.

He absent-mindedly fingered his chin and in doing so had reopened the cut from earlier. She retrieved a damp towel and handed it to him. He looked up as if surprised to find her standing there.

"You look like hell," she said.

"Surely not," he said taking the towel and dabbing delicately at his face.

She laughed. "You're right. It's impossible for you to look like hell. Only you would get tackled face first into the ground and run two miles full tilt and still look debonair."

He smiled as he stood up. "That's the nicest thing anyone has ever said to me." He kissed her cheek and sauntered off to the bath chamber. Maeve could hear him whistling over the rush of the water. She wondered what he had read that had put him into a better mood.

While she had showered, he'd ordered coffee—and replaced the chair back under the knob—so she helped herself to a cup because she figured it was likely going to be a long night. Then she slipped into his vacated spot on the divan. He had taken a pencil from her bag and torn a sheet of notebook paper from the back of her notebook. For a moment she was panicked he may have seen the other things in her satchel— her hotel reservation and travel tickets or the research notes in her notebook, but none of that was necessarily strange or incriminating. He already knew that she was a researcher of some kind. And the agency hadn't left its mark on any of the receipts. She was becoming paranoid. It was easy to slip into easy complacency with Sebastian, but also the two subsequent attacks had really rattled her. The first one was bad enough, although it felt like eons ago, it had been but two days. Her line of work was dangerous, but usually the danger was expected. This had certainly been unexpected.

She heard the shower stop and realized instead of letting her imagination run away with her, she should look at Sebastian's notes so that they could figure out what to do next. He still hadn't led her to the Librae Vitae as her mission required, but even better he had led her to the individual components that would come to eventually make up the Librae Vitae.

Maeve turned her attention to Sebastian's familiar scrawl. He hadn't written much and it was in a mix of French and English. She only knew a handful of words and phrases in French, so she wondered if he'd done that on purpose. More than likely since he was reading in French, it felt natural for him to make his notes in the same language. She knew that sometimes things could get lost in translation. He had only written a handful of items, but the last one was what really caught her attention.

In English, he had written: "I know who you are. And I know that I love you. Yours always."

With trembling hands, she set her coffee cup down and turned. She hadn't heard him come out of the bathroom stealthy as he was. He was standing in the doorway to the bedroom, leaning against the door frame. His black hair was still wet and he hadn't yet put on a shirt. He was as close to an adonis as one could get, but what really took her breath away was the twinkle in his blue eyes and the slow knowing smile that curled his lips.

"Did you think I wouldn't figure it out?"

"I-I don't know what to say," she replied because it was the truth. Her heart was doing a strange rhythmic dance in her chest.

He didn't move, but regarded her intently. The habit was familiar to her and she knew what he expected, what he deserved, so she squarely returned his gaze.

"Tell me how," she demanded now that she was certain he was amused and not mad.

"Silly woman. I would know you anywhere and in any time." He stepped forward into the room and it was like a veil had shifted, revealing more of the Sebastian she knew. Always, he was two steps ahead of her. He was close enough now to kneel in front of her and place his hands around her waist.

Her paranoia had been for naught. Part of her had hoped he'd figure it out, but hope was a fickle thing.

"Only someone who knew me as well as I know myself would be able to think as I do and trust me so implicitly without reason whatsoever. You didn't ask questions and you never seemed surprised by anything—the attacks, Ami, Ludwig—none of it. Then earlier today when I saw you studying me so intently at Ludwig's the look on your face was one of deep caring, not simple concern as if we had only just met. The final confirmation was when you trusted me to catch you when the ladder broke."

She tried to laugh, but it got stuck in her throat. "Well, I didn't exactly have any choice but to trust that you'd catch me."

"Tsk-tsk," Sebastian said. He removed a hand from her waist and cupped her cheek, moving her chin slightly so that she was looking deeply into his eyes. "No, the kind of implicit trust you've shown in me, I know of only one woman who would give that to me and it would be because she had taken a solemn vow to do so. Undoubtedly, you are my wife, Maeve. And I may not understand exactly how at this moment, but I know it to be true. Now tell me everything, my darling, and then we'll figure out what to do about the men trying to kill you."

2093
UNDISCLOSED LOCATION, SPAIN

It was hard to believe it was real. Maeve looked out at the view from the villa. All she could see for miles were green rolling hills surrounding a cerulean blue lake which was cozily nestled in the valley. A breeze blew swirling the white muslin curtains around her shoulders. She stepped through the doors to the terrace and sat down at the small table to enjoy the sun rise and her coffee. She glanced through the open doors. Sebastian was still sprawled across the bed, the sheets twisted around his body like a mummified pharaoh.

She turned back to the picturesque scene in front of her. The sky looked like a Monet painting with shades of lavender, pink and powder blue. The rays of the sun shimmered from behind the hills. She looked down at the delicate golden band on her left ring finger. Engraved on the inside were the Latin words *Tempus est flumen*. Time is a river. It was a play on a Marcus Aurelius quote. Strong is the current of time, no sooner is something brought to you before it's swept away and another takes its place, then this too will be swept away. Over time she had memorized it to her own liking so that she no longer recollected the exact wording.

But the idea had stuck. Time was fleeting and changing and had to be savored and remembered.

***

When Sebastian had first asked her to marry him, she had thought that he was crazy or joking or both. It was a late night and they had been debating the codex. Sebastian had finally conceded to bringing in an expert. This expert was very mysterious but was from Sebastian's network of contacts which Maeve had come to learn—and appreciate—was very vast in the world of antiquities, history, art, and even government. He, she assumed it was he, had been attempting to crack the code for several months. They'd received bits and pieces, but it still wasn't making any sense. Frustrated, Maeve had picked an argument.

"What does it even matter!" she had cried in exasperation. The library was closed and she and Sebastian were alone in his reading room. The remnants of their Italian dinner still spread across the table in front of the fire. "It's been almost two years and we are no closer now than when you first asked me to help you. Maybe we should just give up!"

Instead of taking the bait and engaging in one of their rollicking debates which usually ended in some version of kiss and make up, Sebastian had grown very quiet. He had set his wine glass down and began pacing which set Maeve's nerves on edge.

In truth, her frustration wasn't just with the codex. She truly didn't understand the point especially because it didn't seem that they were getting anywhere, but she was also frustrated that Sebastian had been travelling a lot this past year. He would be gone for months at a time and frankly, Marco hadn't been good company. He had been acting very strangely especially after he had showed her that peculiar room in the tunnels and she hadn't been able to provide him with an answer to its purpose. He had started keeping his distance from her, no longer offering friendly invitations. Oh, sure, he was friendly in a working capacity, but something about him had changed. And she still had never been able to explain the even stranger incident she had witnessed where he seemingly disappeared out of thin air. That wasn't to say she still didn't think about it from time to time.

No, she was frustrated by many things and for the first time since coming to the city two years ago, these past six months were the first she'd felt well and truly alone.

"Well, say something!" She knew she shouldn't take her frustrations out on Sebastian, but she couldn't seem to help herself. She followed him like a moth to a flame and part of her wanted to place the blame—unfairly—for her current depressed feelings onto him.

He looked up then as if just remembering she was still standing there. His expression was startled.

He spread his hands out wide as if in apology.

"Marry me," he said. Just like that. No pomp, no circumstance, no romance.

Maeve deflated a little. This certainly had not been what she was expecting. She had been expecting an argument. Even hoping for one in order to let out the energy of her pent-up frustrations.

"You don't mean that," she said.

Her reaction should have been one of excitement, but she thought he must be joking. She loved Sebastian dearly and knew that he loved her too, but his behavior was completely out of character. It almost seemed like he was hiding something from her. That was probably the most frustrating aspect of all her frustrations.

He closed the space between them and gripped her hands firmly. His face was flushed and his eyes were watery. She'd never seen him this emotional before and she wondered what had happened on his latest trip to make him behave so.

"Oh, I certainly do mean it. Marry me, Maeve Forth. I love you dearly and I trust you more than I've ever trusted anyone else." As if to prove his point he kissed her and she could feel the emotion behind it.

She did want to say yes, but this wasn't how she had imagined Sebastian would propose (if he was going to propose which she had been fairly certain he was going to do so—eventually—Sebastian had his own way of doing things). What she had imagined was a romantic dinner at the French restaurant where he had first taken her and then maybe glasses of wine by a cozy fire...not leftover takeout boxes on the desk and working until two in the morning and arguing about the most impossible text Maeve had ever come across in her life.

"I love you too. This just isn't how I imagined..." She let the words trail off. She had felt silly even saying it.

"What had you imagined?" he looked around as if only just realizing. "Oh, but darling, this is when I love you best. When your mind is churning and you get this little furrow in your brow when you're upset with me." The aforementioned brow then betrayed her just to prove his point. "Just like that."

Her spirit relented and she laughed. "Okay, okay. Yes, Sebastian, I will marry you."

***

That had been three days ago. The days were a whirlwind and it was the first time she had ever travelled with Sebastian. It was also the first time she had ever been out of the country. She'd had no idea that he owned a villa in a small rural town in Spain. She realized then that it was now her villa as well. Maeve Bates. She was not one to hyphenate names or any of that nonsense. You were either all in or all out in her book. The name still sounded strange on her lips.

Sebastian stirred behind her but didn't wake so she took another sip of coffee and turned her attention back to the sun rise behind the hills. Maybe they could go for a swim in the lake today. They'd gotten married yesterday afternoon in the town's small chapel. Besides the priest, there had been only one other witness, a little old woman with a sun worn face and gray hair concealed beneath a delicate bonnet. Her name was Matilde and she was the housekeeper of the villa. Maeve wasn't sure how the woman could upkeep an entire villa on her own, but Sebastian seemed confident in her abilities, and so Maeve was as well. Matilde also didn't speak a lick of English. The one-word Maeve had asked about was what the old woman called Sebastian: *caballero*. When she'd asked him, he'd simply said it meant lord and shrugged his athletic shoulders.

It was refreshing to see Sebastian so far removed from the library and his work. He seemed more relaxed as soon as they'd arrived as if through each time zone a layer of responsibility had been shed. His manner became easier and he joked more not only with her, but with the locals in the town. He walked around the villa barefoot, his feet slapping across the limestone. Before the wedding ceremony, from the balcony of the villa she'd spied him swimming in the lake and when he emerged onto the sandy bank she'd realized he was *desnudo*. Here he was completely at ease.

There certainly was a sense of freedom about the place.

However, she still sensed that there was something he wanted to tell her. She had no doubt he would do so when the timing was right. Right for him anyways. She also knew that whatever he wanted to tell her, he had wanted her faithful vow of devotion before doing so. She did not take that lightly.

There was a rustle of bed sheets and Sebastian slipped through the doors to the balcony. His sable hair was messed from sleep and he was blurry eyed, so she poured him a cup of coffee. He nodded his head in thanks and sat down across from her his eyes fixed on the sunrise as it finally crested the green hills and glistened off the pristine blue of the lake.

They sat in companionable silence for almost a quarter of an hour and Maeve didn't mind one bit. Sebastian was as reflective as she, if not more so.

Finally, he set his coffee down and stretched. When his arms came down, he took her hand from across the table.

"I don't think I've ever felt more at peace than I have these past few days."

"This place is magical," she replied.

"Yes, it is. But it's not just the place. It's you. My wife." His thumb brushed the band on her finger. His matched and had the same saying engraved inside. The bands were simple and elegant. "I cannot tell you what a relief it is to have someone I can finally trust. You're beautiful and brilliant. I am a lucky man."

He intertwined his fingers with hers.

His sapphire blue eyes were intense.

"I have to tell you something."

"I know, darling," she replied. Placing her coffee cup down she reached across the table for his other hand and intertwined her fingers with his.

He laughed, a deep bubbling sound. "Of course you do. I would expect nothing less from my other half." Then his smile subsided, but before he could go on, Maeve interrupted.

"It won't change my mind. Whatever it is."

"Oh, I know that. You need not convince me there. It's not so much that I think it will change your mind, it's that I fear you won't know what to do with the information."

She didn't tell him that she already had an inkling. All of that research. The obsession with the Libre Vitae. However, her theory had been slightly off, so her surprise was genuine when Sebastian ungracefully blurted out: "I'm immortal!" He squeezed her hand and hurried to continue. "I mean, I can die from a fatal wound. However, it's not likely until I am of a certain age and the regenerative properties in my RNA are degraded enough to hinder healing."

Dawning finally settled into Maeve's laten brain as the pieces finally clicked into place.

"That's why you're so obsessed with the Libre Vitae—it isn't because you want to find out how to live forever..."

Sebastian nodded. "It's because I want to find out how to undo it."

2093
NEW YORK CITY, UNITED STATES

Maeve kept her wedding band on a long chain around her neck, so that it was always close to her heart. It wasn't going to be easy to keep her marriage to Sebastian a secret. The ring if found could easily be explained away as having belonged to her birth mother or even a purchase from an antiques dealer or pawn shop. There were numerous explanations of which she could imagine. But wearing it around her ring finger would be a dead giveaway.

Sebastian had agreed to keep his own wedding band in his personal vault, but he hadn't liked it one bit. She had convinced him—after his revelation—that the plan she had begun to concoct would fail if anyone knew—besides the priest and

Spanish housekeeper, of course—that they were husband and wife. Before they had left Spain, he had found a local tattooist and had a small Egyptian Ankh tattooed on his chest near his heart. It was a simple looped cross. If anyone saw it, it would just seem to be reflective of his love for travel and of Egypt in particular.

The Egyptian symbol for eternal life was common enough and appeared in many Egyptian murals and texts. However, to a scholar, the symbol held a little more meaning. The circle was representative of a woman and the cross representative of a man, together it represented the unification of man and woman. It was Sebastian's subtle acknowledgement—or she supposed not so subtle if his shirt was off—of his wife.

As soon as Sebastian had revealed his heart to her, the secret that he carried around and had never told anyone, she knew why he had wanted the assurance of her commitment. But she also knew their marriage showed his implicit trust in her to not only keep his secret, but to help him figure out how to undo it. It was a weighty task and she was sincerely flattered that he found her a capable partner.

She stared out the window of her office as she recalled the relief in his sapphirine eyes once he had finally confessed over coffee in Spain. Afterward, he'd had Mathilde bring them plates of *tortilla de patatas* (essentially omelets) and *ensaïmada* (really, she could never get enough of fried dough and powdered sugar of any variety) to the little table on their terrace. It was a sweet ending to what Maeve had perceived as a bitter tale.

Her heart had ached for the man seated across from her.

His story had made her angry on his behalf. She wasn't naïve, she knew that after the war horrific things were still happening all over the world and that she'd been fortunate to be born to a kind birthing mother who had wanted a child to raise a little while and encouraged her schooling and education. Not all were as fortunate as she had been.

It was a complete violation of humanity to experiment unwittingly on anyone, but especially on children who were the most innocent of society. Eugenics had been around for over a hundred years at that point and that was only in its modern iteration after the Second World War. However, that didn't mean that government sponsored institutions and private institutions had stopped the practice. What government wouldn't want to make the perfect soldier? Who wouldn't want to create the perfect child? What person wouldn't want to live forever? Maeve could think of plenty of people who wouldn't want any of those things, but that didn't stop the powerful or the wealthy from trying. How many unwitting victims were created in the process? How many lives sacrificed?

No, there had to be something that she could do. She had to help Sebastian—her husband—undo what had been done to him. At the very least she would help him find the answers he sought.

There was a knock on her office door. The person didn't wait for her to confirm her presence which meant that it was Marco. Sebastian wouldn't bother to knock and most other people didn't even know that the office existed hidden on the half floor as it was.

"Hey stranger," he smiled entering the room and closing the door behind him. They still worked with one another on occasion, but as Sebastian had pulled her into more research, her cataloguing of materials had taken a secondary priority. She felt on edge at Marco's presence, but decided to shake it off.

They were friends—they had spent that one lonely Christmas together—and even if he didn't bring her into his confidence and didn't understand her relationship with Sebastian, she was willing to let bygones be bygones.

"Hi there." She gestured to the open chair at the table, but Marco shook his head.

"I just wanted to pop in and say hello. I haven't seen you in a while. You look…different." She did look different. Spain had been as good for her as it had been for Sebastian and she felt that the institution of marriage was also suiting her just fine.

"I'll take that as a compliment. Yes, I had a much-needed vacation and feel quite refreshed. Thanks for noticing. How have you been?" She picked up her mug and sipped her coffee which had gone lukewarm as she had gotten lost in her thoughts.

"Good, good. Same old. You know I've been thinking…I never did figure out what that strange room was for. Did you ever come up with anything?" He quickly added, "I know you're always researching and thought maybe you'd come across something."

It wasn't the most elegant segue but since she was letting bygones be bygones, she decided to be at least partially honest with him. "The icons on that banner were the only thing that caught my interest. A mix of Templar and Egyptian symbology, but together they have no meaning to me. The tunnels have been there for hundreds of years. There are networks of tunnels beneath cities all over the world. I can't say that I'm surprised. But I am surprised that that particular room was so easy to get into. Almost as if…"

"We were meant to find it," Marco finished. "I thought the same thing."

The barrier he'd put up the past few months since that incident slid down slightly. Maeve wanted to ask about that day when she saw him disappear out of thin air outside her window, but she didn't want him to slide that barrier back up. Sebastian was her husband, but Marco was her only friend.

"Yes, but who would want you to find such a thing? And why?"

Marco nodded in agreement. "There are still too many questions." He looked down at that peculiar timepiece and Maeve had to bite her lip to keep from commenting. "I should get going. A delivery is scheduled to arrive any minute and I really did just want to say hello."

"I understand. Thanks for stopping by. And, Marco, don't be a stranger. Your company is always welcome." She meant the words, so she smiled when she said them.

He paused at the door and turned. "You know there is something…There's an organization I do volunteer work for. I was wondering if you'd be interested…"

She nodded. "Sure, I'd love to check it out."

"Great. I'll get something set up." He smiled, looked down at his watch again with a furrowed brow, and exited her office.

Hurriedly, she slipped off her shoes so she was in her socks and waited a few beats before she slipped out her office door after him.

Marco was walking briskly, but she saw his brown head as he passed through the stacks of books. She trotted silently to follow him, periodically hiding between the book cases as he walked. At the end of one row, he turned into a doorway and she could just make out his form in the dimness. She crouched down at the end of a row of bookcases and watched.

He looked down at his watch and the black face lit up turning his face a ghastly green. Then he tapped at the face a few times and that's when it happened. He was just gone. This time she knew that her eyes had not played tricks on her. She waited a few seconds then tiptoed into the doorway.

It was a supply closet full of towels and a mop bucket. It was a small closet, barely room for a person to fit inside. And Marco was no longer there. There wasn't even any evidence that he had been there only seconds before. She didn't know what she had just witnessed. But she knew that she had to find out. Marco was up to something and she suspected that it had to do with whatever he did for *'volunteer work.'*

2094
UNDISCLOSED LOCATION, UNITED STATES

"Do you have any questions Agent Forth?"

The man was void of facial expressions. The only hint of emotion was the fluttering of the ends of his bushy gray mustache. His eyes were a cold steel and his jaw looked like it had been cut from granite. Bushy gray eyebrows set over the steel flints complemented the mustache.

Maeve shifted uncomfortably in her chair. It was a very hard chair and she had been sitting in it for nearly two hours. When she had finally confronted Marco about his disappearing act, she thought that he would bluff or laugh it off, but he hadn't. He'd looked abashed for a moment. To be fair, she had backed him up against a set of bookcases as they had been cataloguing a shipment. Her plan had been to catch him off guard, so that he wouldn't be able to come up with a lie.

And she had succeeded in catching him off guard. She could tell from the dilation of his pupils in his hazel eyes, but he'd recovered quickly—too quickly. As if he could slow his parasympathetic nervous system on command. She was standing close enough to notice the decrease in the rise and fall of his chest. She had him cornered though and there was no getting out of it. He couldn't run as that would be an admission of some kind of guilt, besides on his right side he had been blocked in by a stack of shipping crates and on his left was the end of the aisle which dead-ended into a wall.

What she hadn't been expecting was for him to turn it back on her so quickly. He'd admitted it had to do with his *volunteer work*—said with the slightest bit of hesitancy—and that he really wanted to introduce her to the organization. He hadn't explained what it was and she figured she'd find out soon enough. What it was she never could have even hazarded a guess remotely close. It was the stuff of a science fiction novel.

Marco worked for the government in a secret program called Operation Khonsu—the Egyptian god of time. And that he was part of a team of time travelling agents. The mysterious watches used a crystalized radioactive ingredient called Murex that could, put simply, fold the fabric of space time. Their Opus Mission was to prevent a charismatic political leader from taking power—not just of the United States, but of the world—by creating stitches, or subtle changes, to the past timeline to influence both the present and the future.

Apparently, Marco had been taken by Maeve's sharp intellect and ability to assimilate information almost immediately, but he had to get to know her a bit better before he could tell if she would be a fit for his team. A team that was working very closely to prevent this leader from coming into power. She hadn't asked why there was an opening on his team, but she suspected it had to do with, excuse the pun, someone's untimely demise. When she asked about his disappearing act, it was the perfect opportunity to bring her in for an interview—and an extensive screening.

As she learned more about the program and its mission an uneasy feeling had come over her. She hadn't even actually agreed to join the organization, but once Marco brought her into the fold—a sterile unassuming office building in a struggling village in the city that was still trying to get re-established after the Third World War—she realized that an agent didn't choose the agency as much as the agency chose the agent.

Seemingly unrelated things began to fall into place. Marco working at the Bates Library for International Studies. The carefully placed ad for employment. Marco trying to dissuade her from engaging in a relationship with Sebastian. His disappearing—which she now knew was time travel—in and out of the library at random. The strange room in the tunnels, which she now saw with fresh eyes as a chance for him to assess her ability to handle unexpected situations but also her ability to discern information. Would she jump to conclusions? Think through it rationally? And then there was the way he carefully and patiently had earned her trust. She wasn't mad at Marco. She didn't even feel betrayed by him. Some other preservation instinct had begun to take over as she saw the last pieces of the puzzle coming together.

So, when Agent Z—the steely eyed gentleman—pushed an 8.5 x 11 photo across the desk in her direction to show the

Opus Mission's main target her own expression was granite and didn't even register the faintest hint of surprise.

A familiar face with wavy black hair and sapphirine eyes looked back at her. His skin was tanned and he wasn't smiling, but there was a slight upward curve at the corners of his mouth. He was older than she knew him, the slightest flecks of salt in that pepper-colored hair. But she'd come to know that face as well as her own. However, she also knew that heart as well as her own and after Sebastian told her about his—Ailment? Affliction? —she knew that very bad people were involved and that the best way she could help her husband was to infiltrate those bad people. So here she was pretending she felt nothing as her husband's glittering eyes looked back at her.

She pretended to stare for a minute at the face then she carefully used her fingertips to push the photo back across the desk.

Agent Z was a man of few words and without additional comment he handed her a small leather folio. Inside were a stack of papers—passports, fake identifications, money in several different currencies, and a watch. She pulled the watch out. It was simple—almost like a bracelet. Much more discreet than Marco's. She clasped it around her left wrist and the face glinted like an onyx mirror in the sterile light.

She wasn't nervous about infiltrating the agency. But she was nervous about keeping a secret from the man she loved and who had bared his soul to her. However, if it would ultimately protect him from harm then it was worth the risk. She picked up the portfolio and stood understanding that the interview was now over.

"No, Sir. No questions."

2095
LONDON, ENGLAND

Maeve wasn't certain what she had expected when she entered the shop, but this was not it. An older gentleman stood behind the counter. He was nearly a full head shorter than she was and had white hair that curled behind his ears. Half his face was obscured by a bushy white beard and mustache, but expressive eyebrows hung low over his eyes which were an ambiguous shade of hazel. He appeared to be in his fifties and wore a battered tan cardigan sweater that had a hole near one of the elbows.

He regarded her over the top of his glasses which had slid to the tip of his pointed nose. She made her way around the periphery of the store keeping one wary eye on him and one eye inspecting the merchandise. The shop was full of antiquities from art to jewelry to odds and ends. In fact, that was the name: *From Odds to Ends*. She thought it was fitting because she hadn't seen quite so diverse a collection under any one roof except for maybe in a museum.

The letter had been unmarked. It had come addressed to her home in New York City. Sebastian and she had thought it prudent to continue to live as they had been before marriage in order to better keep their relationship hidden. The letter had been typed on a typewriter using thick cream-colored paper and folded into thirds. Inside the envelope had been a receipt for a room at a small inn in London and a passenger boat ticket for two weeks from the date she had read the letter. Most importantly, the letter had contained directions to a specific store—From Odds to Ends—as well as a date and time to be there. She knew better than to ignore a summons like this one, even if she wasn't exactly sure who had sent it.

Friend or foe?

Her heart was pounding in her chest and she bent over to inspect a small malachite statue of the Egyptian goddess Hathor. The horned goddess of love and fertility. Without even picking it up to inspect it, she could see that it was exquisitely hand carved. She didn't know who she was looking for and was simply banking on the fact that he—or she—would make their presence known to her.

Finally, the little man came hurrying over to her from behind the counter. "*Gutentag, Frau! Bonjour madam!*"

She looked up. How had he known that she was married? Her hand instinctively went to the necklace hidden beneath her sweater. Hopefully, it looked as if he had startled her and didn't draw suspicion.

"*Parlez-vous anglais, monsieur?*"

She knew very little French and even less German.

His eyes softened. "Yes, indeed! I was afraid you wouldn't come!" He bustled away whistling and she realized that he meant for her to follow him.

They wound their way down the end aisle, past the front shop door which the little man locked and flipped his sign to read closed, before continuing down the opposite aisle and along the far wall to a door in the back that had those old-fashioned western saloon swinging doors. One hung precariously from its hinges.

She followed him to the back room which was wall-to-wall shelves of boxes, books, art, and antiquities. There was barely any room to walk. Her heart was still pounding, but she figured if things really went south that she would be able to overpower the little man. She had nearly a foot on him and probably at least thirty pounds.

They finally reached a small wooden desk that was buried beneath boxes and papers. From the ornately carved legs though, Maeve could see that it was old and it was made of mahogany. Desks weren't made like that anymore. The little man elbowed his way past some piles that were stacked as tall as he was before going round to the chair behind the desk. He gestured at a chair that was loaded with a stack of file folders and Maeve carefully removed them and set them on one of the few clear spaces on the floor nearby.

Once they were seated, she noticed there was an elaborate pink floral tea pot on a small tray and two matching tea cups with gold rims sitting on the edge of the desk. It had been hidden behind a haphazard stack of papers. He poured two cups, whistling through his teeth while he did so. She accepted her cup, but waited until he drank from his own before taking a sip from from her own cup. It was room temperature but she didn't mind.

He set down his cup. "You don't remember me, do you?"

"Should I? Remember you?"

He laughed and it was a cheerful sound. It would be just her luck that her murderer would be a cute little grandpa of an old man with a cheerful laugh. The universe was peculiar in that way.

"I suppose not! Wishful thinking, I guess! I met you once in Luxor!"

"But I've never been to Luxor," Maeve replied truthfully. Was this some kind of scam? A set up?

"Ah, well. I suppose. I'm not sure how much to say, *Frauline Forth*. Or is it *Frau Bates*?" One of those white eyebrows arched suspiciously high.

"Who are you?" She set her teacup down and folded her hands in her lap. She hoped that he didn't see the tremor of her hand.

"A friend you can trust! I knew you once...in my past, but I suppose for you it was your present and maybe now it is your future!"

The man wasn't making any sense. She was starting to doubt his sanity. And here she was alone in a back room in a locked shop with him. Drinking tea. That could have been poisoned. What on earth was she thinking? She wasn't thinking though. *She was trusting.*

"Will you at least tell me your name since you seem to know so much about me?"

"Ludwig Hoffman!"

He had surprised her again. She had read about the German ex-pat Egyptian archaeologist. There had been an accident on one of his digs and some workers had died. He had given up his archaeological passions after that and some say he had even gone a little mad afterwards. While she had wondered about his insanity momentarily, she recognized the lucidity in his hazel eyes and knew that this man was indeed quite sane. She probably had met him—just not yet. And if he knew of her relationship with Sebastian, which no one at least in this era did, then he must be an ally.

"You are correct, Dr. Hoffman. My title is the latter."

He grinned. "I hope you realize that means that I am trustworthy! Because I have a very important gift for you!"

Amongst the chaos of his desk there was a long narrow box. He pushed it towards her now. She carefully lifted the lid suddenly overcome with the realization that she knew exactly what she would find inside. The box was satin lined and inside laid a gold watch with an opalescent face absent of numbers. There were rubies, emeralds and sapphire gems winking at her as if to say: "And you thought you'd never see us again!" She reached down into the box and turned the watch over to see faint wedge-shaped markings engraved on the back.

Ludwig handed her a magnifying glass. Four years ago, she wouldn't have been able to read the peculiar markings that were not pictorial like hieroglyphics, but also not the bold lines of Hebrew or the flowing strokes of Arabic. But now she could just make out the wedge-shaped markings as cuneiform—the first known written language.

"This too will be swept away," she read. It was the continuation of the quote inside her wedding band. *Time is a sort of river of passing events, and strong is its current; no sooner is a thing brought to sight than it is swept by and another takes its place, and this too will be swept away.* Marcus Aurelius wasn't from the same era of cuneiform by about 3500 years. The watch was beautiful, but not created in antiquity although to an undiscerning eye, it would look as though it had been. To someone unfamiliar or unable to read the strange characters on the back, and without the proper context, it would appear as old as a medieval chalice.

Her eyes moved to the leather satchel of tools laying open on the desk. She looked up at Ludwig finally understanding. She undid the watch at her left wrist and handed it to him.

"I knew you'd understand!" He beamed. He made quick work of it. Picking up a small screw driver he undid the back of her watch and then removed the back of the gold watch. Inside of her watch next to the circuit board was a small area that sparkled in the low light of the room. Using tweezers, Ludwig carefully picked up a portion of the substance. There was a small open space next to the gold watch's circuit board that matched her own watch's circuit board and Ludwig used the tweezers to deposit the substance into the open compartment. With sure hands he then reassembled the backs to both of the watches.

"You're a jeweler now." Her palms were sweating but her tone was light.

Ludwig shrugged as he handed her back the watch that allowed her to move through time.

"I'm a man of many talents! After I.... well. I don't want to give you too much information. But I finally got the help I needed from a dear friend very familiar to you! He helped me establish this shop after I got my health in order once again." As he said this, he tucked the watch back inside the satin lining of the box and replaced its lid. "I'm afraid that you're going to have to be the one to deliver it."

She nodded. She would have to go back to 2091 to ensure that it was at the library when she was there sorting through the deliveries and cataloguing the items coming into the collection. Then she remembered something—an important detail.

"Wait! There's one more thing." She saw a scroll of thick papyrus sticking out from the edge of the pile of papers on the corner of Ludwig's desk and tore a piece off. Ludwig didn't object, instead he handed her a pen.

Even though it had been four years she remembered exactly what she was supposed to write. Now she knew why she had written it in French—not many people were multilingual anymore and that little Parisienne café had been the beginning of their relationship. Not to mention it was the language of lovers so it seemed doubly appropriate. Satisfied she put the pen down and tucked the little piece of papyrus into the box beneath the satin lining.

She stood. "Thank you, Dr. Hoffman. You don't know what this means for us."

His smile shone through his beard. "Oh, I think I do, Frau Bates. If you ever need a friend…just know that I am here. I hope you enjoy my first and your second meeting—it's a day that I won't soon forget."

She couldn't explain why, but she felt her eyes welling with tears. She reached over and patted the older man's tanned wrinkled hand. "I look forward to it."

Besides, she'd always wanted to go to Egypt.

And with that she looked down and pressed her watch face. She set the year to 2091 and the location to New York City. She had a package to deliver.

The last thing she remembered was Ludwig's smiling face before the small room faded to black and she felt as if the world was once again spinning. She clutched the small box to her chest as she hurtled back through time. What she did now would echo in eternity and she'd be damned if she'd let them destroy the man she loved more than time itself.

Time is a sort of river of passing events, and strong is its current; no sooner is a thing brought to sight than it is swept by and another takes its place, and this too will be swept away.

AUTHOR'S NOTE

The nice thing about setting a book in the future is letting my imagination run wild. This book is a work of fiction and while some places may be initially based in reality, they've been highly fictionized into a futuristic post-apocalyptic vision. Any language errors are strictly my own as are any inconsistencies in the science of space-time travel. However, *die glocke* was indeed real. Unfortunately, Xerum 525, commonly known as Murex, is not and is simply a product of my own creation. The author both credits and blames her overactive imagination for any other mistakes, errors, or omissions.

ACKNOWLEDGEMENTS

First and foremost, I am thankful to God, my creator who incarnated on earth to live amongst his creation. The creativity and imagination He has gifted to me has been both my greatest achievement and sometimes my own curse (overactive imagination, ahem).

Copious amounts of gratitude to my dad who is always willing to bounce around ideas and helps me to edit all of my books. The books have gotten further and fewer between than when I was doing five in a year, but I'm older and more tired now!

Also, always grateful for my sweet angel baby, Sunshine Ivy, who is a comfort to me and curls up on her chaise with Lambie while I write, edit, and generally create. I am so thankful that God entrusted you to my care and me into yours. Rescue is my favorite breed.

ABOUT THE AUTHOR

Jennifer L. Kelly currently is a digital marketing professional extraordinaire. In a past life, she was a middle school teacher, a production coordinator for a materials science society, and a wizard at making candles. She currently resides in Ohio not far from the shores of Lake Erie.

When she isn't writing, she can be found flying through space time in the TARDIS with the Doctor, hanging out in the Gryffindor Common Room, or tackling her never-ending TBR list.

She is the author of the YA dystopian series The Lucia Chronicles and the YA fantasy sci-fi series The Elementals. Visit her website www.jenniferlkelly.com to learn more.

BOOKS BY
JENNIFER L. KELLY

Young Adult

House of Snakes Trilogy
House of Snakes
Sword & Air
Princess of Darkness

The Lucia Chronicles Trilogy
The Prophecy
The Dissentient
The Beacon
The Girl Who Wasn't Loved
(Novella)

The Elementals Series
Army of Fire
The Earth Key
Genesis of Wood
The Water Queen
Secret of Metal
A Vessel for Darkness
(Novella)

Standalone Women's Fiction

The Fractured Life of Jenny
McClain
A Heart That Blooms

Children's Books

Lizzy or Liz, Never Elizabeth
and the Unbirthday
Lizzy or Liz, Never Elizabeth
and the Peanut Kid
The Moon People

Non-Fiction

Living Authentically

Coloring Book

Mind Power: An A-Z
Coloring Book of Positivity